# Little Flower Folks

This edition published 2025
by Living Book Press
Copyright © Living Book Press, 2025

ISBN:    978-1-76153-680-9 (hardcover)
         978-1-76153-692-2 (softcover)

First published in 1892.

A catalogue record for this book is available from the National Library of Australia

# Little Flower Folks

or Stories From Flowerland for the Home and School

## Volume 2

by

Mara Louise Pratt-Chadwick

# Contents

# At School Again!

NEARLY two months of vacation! And here we all are again in the old schoolroom. "Why, I feel like a grown-up, very old person who had travelled all over the world and had been gone for years and years," said Allie with a deep sigh.

"You haven't lost even a wee bit of your imagination, Allie, I am sure," laughed one of the "big girls," throwing her arms about Allie in an enthusiastic school-girl hug.

"My, but won't we have wonders to tell our teachers about our vacation! I wonder if she will remember that she asked us to bring home some flowers?"

"Remember? Of course, she will," answered Harry. "She never makes believe to us. And if she said she wanted us to bring flowers, she meant it, and she'll remember. I—"

"Thank you, Harry," said the teacher coming up just then; "I am glad you and I can trust each other so fully."

Harry blushed furiously, as much with honest pleasure as with embarrassment. Then followed such a rush of greetings! Everybody was so glad to see everybody else that it was a full five minutes past the school hour before we were settled in our seats.

On the desk stood a great bouquet of rich, red Jacquemi-not roses and pure white lilies with a little card attached on which were these words:

*"Greeting to our Teacher from the Botany Class."*

Such a happy color came in her face as her eyes fell upon the flowers. She said nothing, but opening the Bible she read to us these words: "Consider the lilies of the field, how they grow. They toil not, neither do they spin. And yet I say unto you that even Solomon in all his glory was not arrayed like one of these."

And then from Longfellow she read:

### SANDALPHON

He gathers the prayers as he stands
And they change into flowers in his hands.
    Into garlands of purple and red;
And beneath the great arch of the portal
Through the streets of the City Immortal
    Is wafted the fragrance they shed.

It is but a legend, I know —
A fable, a phantom, a show
    Of the ancient Rabbinical lore;
Yet the old mediaeval tradition
The beautiful strange superstition,
    But haunts me and holds me the more.

When I look from my window at night,
And the welkin above is all white,
    All throbbing and panting with stars,
Above them majestic is standing
Sandalphon the angel, expanding
    His pinions in nebulous bars.

And the legend, I feel, is a part
Of the hunger and thirst of the heart,
    The frenzy and fire of the brain,
That grasps at the fruitage forbidden
The golden pomegranates of Eden,
    To quiet its fever and pain.

# Flowers from Nova Scotia, Mount Tom, and Long Island

IN due time, we had our first Flower lesson for the fall term. It was not like any lesson we had had before. So many flowers were brought from different localities where we had visited during the long summer vacation, and there was so much general information to be given and taken regarding our journeys and our adventures, that our teacher really feared an all-night session would hardly hear us through.

There were Kittie and Ned whose father had taken them on a sea voyage to Nova Scotia. Such reports Ned had of life on shipboard! His vessel had been saluted by Her Majesty's squadron just as it was about to enter the port of Halifax! The Lieutenant Governor had paid their vessel a visit and had invited Ned and Kittie to pay him a visit! They had attended church at such a quaint, old, moss-covered stone church, had visited an English college, and had sailed on such a beautiful lake — La Rosignal!

Ned had brought some beautiful agates and amethysts, and Kittie had some flowers from the shores of the lake. They were the little Monesis or "Our Delight," members of the Wintergreen group, but seldom found in the United States. There were enough, all nicely pressed, for each one of us; and it was with the air of real curiosity collectors that we fastened them into our blank books, and a note beneath:

MONESIS or OUR DELIGHT.
*Flowers from the shores of Lake La Rosignal, Nova Scotia. Gathered by Ned and Kittie Brown.*

Lizzie had some flowers, too. During the summer, she had climbed up the rough sides of Mount Tom and had found growing among the rugged rocks and hid away in the clefts these little blue flowers.

"Blue Harebells!" said our teacher. "They belong to the Bellworts — you remember we talked of a Bellwort last spring — alternate leaves *without* stipules, a superior calyx which does not fall off, a regular bell-like corolla five-cleft, five stamens with distinct anthers, a two-celled ovary adhering to the calyx, a style covered with little fine hairs and—"

"We have a h-a-i-r-bell!" shouted Harry. "True," answered the teacher when we had done laughing at Harry's enthusiasm, "but this happens to be a h-a-r-e-bell. It seems too bad to lose your pointed application, Harry, but perhaps you will accept this occasion for the flower's name in place of yours. In the old English days, when, as I told you, people believed much in the fairies, this little bell-shaped flower was considered a fairy bell; and one ventured to add that one night at midnight, as he was travelling across the moor, he heard a little tinkling sound. The sound drawing nearer and nearer, he stopped

4

HAREBELL.

to listen. Suddenly there rushed by a little hare, a tiny blue bell fastened about his neck. 'Whither so fast, little hare?' called the traveller. 'Do not stop me,' answered the little hare; 'I am bound on an important errand from the queen of fairyland!' And from that time the little blue-bell flower was called the Hare-bell."

"I think I like your name the best," laughed Harry, shaking his curly head. "See what a funny plant Jack has found. Looks to me just like a piece of old saffron-colored yarn."

"Dodder-plant! Poor, miserable looking vine! It is called a *Parasite*, that is, a plant that lives on another plant. It

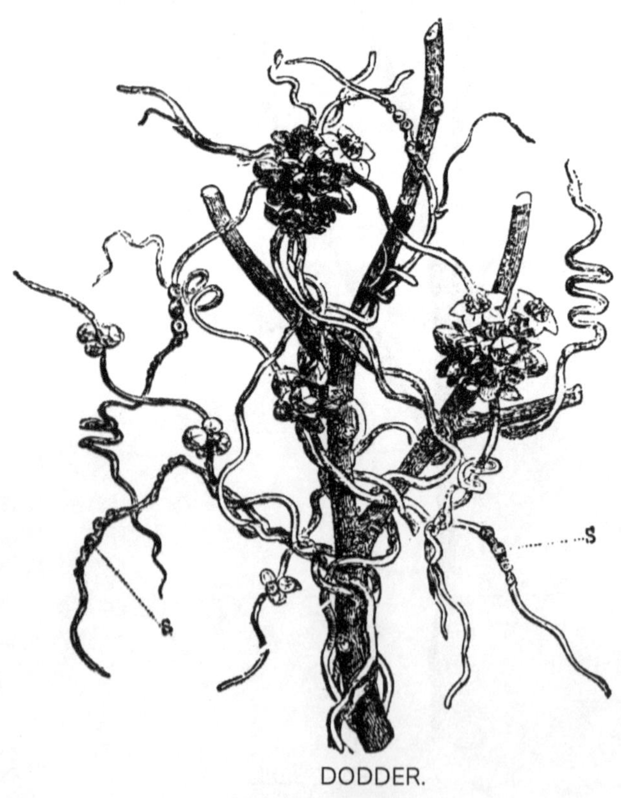

DODDER.

starts out from the ground in the first place like any plant. By and by, as if too lazy to live of itself, it withers at its root, twines itself about any shrub or herb that chances to be within reach, and seems to get its support from that plant. I have known some people who might well be named Dodders, judging from the lazy way in which they seem content to live upon their friends and relatives.

"Remember this word — Parasite — for you will often

BENDWEED.

hear it outside of botany as well as in botany. I wonder if we have any parasites in this schoolroom? Have we anyone here who is too lazy to do his own work; who 'sponges,' as you boys say, his answers from anybody who will help him; who expects his teacher to put knowledge into his head while he sits yawning; who expects his father to clothe him and his mother to feed him and his sister to wait upon him while he does nothing at all? Such a boy as that is a

SWEET POTATO.

real parasite; and you may be sure he will grow up just such a weak good-for-nothing as the floral parasite is."

"I brought these," said Ella, as the teacher called for other flowers, "from Long Island. They seem like our Morning Glories, but I thought I'd bring them because they were from another locality."

"They are not quite Morning Glories, after all, Ella, though they are sisters, both belonging to the Convolvulus Family. These are Bindweeds. They used once to be called Morning Glories, but on account of these two little bracts which you see at the base of the calyx, botanists call them by a new name — Calystegia — meaning calyx-covering."

"Examine the calyx hidden away in these bracts, and you will find it five-parted. The bell-like corolla has five folds, and the ovary has one cell with four seeds. Another difference from the Morning Glory is that the leaves, though heart-shaped, are rather arrow-shaped at their base. The leaves of the Morning Glory are not at all arrow-like."

"The Cypress vine is also a sister of the Morning Glory; and there is one other sister, very useful and very domestic in her tastes — the Batatas or Sweet Potato."

"And now for our next lessons with our flower friends, bring whatever you happen to find," said our teacher as we mounted the dried Bindweeds in our books. "Now that you are learning to describe carefully, we can move on with quite a little speed over these fall flowers. We must try not to lose or overlook a single one."

# THE ANXIOUS LEAF.

Once upon a time, a little leaf was heard to sigh and cry, as leaves do when a gentle wind is about.

"What is the matter, little leaf?" said the twig.

"The wind has just told me that someday it will pull me off and throw me down to die on the ground," sobbed the little leaf.

The twig told it to the branch on which it grew, and the branch told it to the tree; and when the tree heard it, it rustled all over, and sent back word to the leaf: "Do not be afraid; hold on tightly, and you shall not go till you want to."

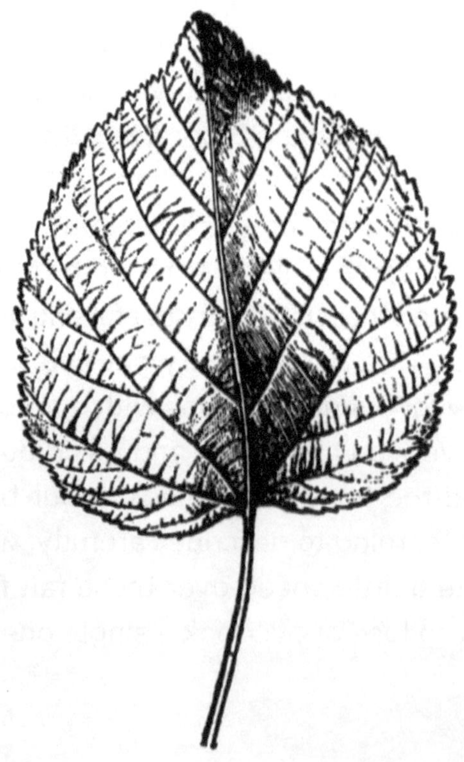

So the leaf stopped sighing and went on rustling and singing. Every time the tree shook itself and stirred up all its leaves, the branches shook themselves, and the little twig shook itself; and the little leaf danced up and down merrily, as if nothing could ever pull it off.

And so it grew all summer long and till October. And when the bright days of autumn came, the little leaf saw all the leaves around becoming very beautiful. Some were yellow and some scarlet, and some striped with both colors. Then it asked the tree what it meant.

And the tree said: "All these leaves are getting ready to fly away; and they have put on these beautiful colors because of joy." Then the little leaf began to want to go and grew very beautiful in thinking of it, and when it was very gay in color, saw that the branches of the tree had no color in them and so the leaf said, "Oh, branches! Why are you lead-color, and we golden?"

"We must keep on our work-clothes, for our life is not done; but your clothes are for holiday, because your tasks are over." Just then a little puff of wind came, and the leaf let go without thinking of it; and the wind took it up and turned it over and over, and whirled it like a spark of fire in the air; and then it dropped gently down under the edge of the fence among hundreds of leaves, and fell into a dream, and never waked up to tell what it dreamed about.

- H. W. BEECHER

# Our Analysis Chart. - 1.

ON the following Friday afternoon, we found, on entering our schoolroom, a chart hanging upon the wall. We knew it had something to do with our Botany, for on the cover was written, "Key to the Treasure House of the Flowers." Then too, on the board beside it, was a long list of dubious-looking words, so long and hard, evidently having something to do with Botany.

"Whew!" whistled Harry as his eye fell upon the list.

"Don't cross a bridge until you come to it," said the teacher, laughing at the despairing expression on Harry's face. "And remember the lions that so frightened the traveler because, *at the distance*, he could not see that they were merely *iron lions*."

After our reading lesson and our language lesson, we were ready to attack the lions, if such they were to prove.

Here is the list as they looked upon the board. So many of them we already knew that, after all, the lesson was no harder than our everyday spelling lessons; and it was far more interesting.

*Ex o gen*
*End o gen*

———————————

*Pol y pet a lous*
*Mon o pet a lous*
*A pet a lous*

---

*Spadix-like*
*Petal-like*
*Husk-like*

---

*Cor ol la*
*Sta mens*
*Pis til*
*Ca lyx*
*Se pals*

---

*Cot y le dons*
*Cat kins*

---

"Now," said our teacher going to the chart, and lifting the cover, "on the first page of our chart we see:"

## GREAT CLASSES

**I. ENDOGENS.**
> *Stem has fibers in threads.*
> *Leaves parallel-veined.*
> *Flowers in threes or sixes, never in fives.*
> *One cotyledon.*

**II. EXOGENS.**
> *Stem has pith in the center.*
> *Leaves netted-veined.*
> *Flowers in fives or fours, rarely in threes.*
> *Two cotyledons.*

"From this page, we are to learn that all the plants we shall have to do with will belong to one of these two great classes - Endogens or Exogens. Therefore, the first thing we shall do today with this little flower we are to analyze is to decide to which of these two classes it belongs.

"The leaves alone will tell the story. Are the veins netted or parallel?"

"Netted-veined," we answered in a chorus. "And I see the flowers are in fives. The cotyledons we do not know about, neither do we need to know just now; and the stem, you can readily see, has a pithy center. Therefore we know that this plant belongs to which one of the great classes?"

"Exogens," we shouted again, delighted with the mysterious unfolding of our chart.

"Now, if our plant had been an Endogen, we should have turned to the page with the heading *Endogen*; but as it was not, we do not need that page but rather this one with the heading *Exogen*." And so speaking, the chart was opened to a page like this:

**EXOGENS.**
*Apetalous.*
*Monopetalous.*
*Polypetalous.*

"Having decided that our plant is an Exogen, we must next decide whether it is Apetalous, Monopetalous, or Polypetalous."

"Polypetalous!" cried Harry.

"Be careful, my boy! Look more closely."

"It's like those Bluets we examined in the spring," answered Harry a moment later, this time less noisily. "These divisions at the top are all united into one tube-shaped corolla; and the flower is monopetalous."

"That is better," answered the teacher. "Now let us turn our chart again to the page with Monopetalous for its heading."

**2. MONOPET-ALOUS.**

- **COROLLA ON THE SEED-CRADLE.**
  - Honeysuckle
  - Mirabilis
  - Madder
  - Campanula
  - Huckleberry
  - Composite
  - Lobelia
  - Gourd
  - Teasel
  - Valerian

- **COROLLA BELOW THE SEED-CRADLE**
  - *More Stamens than Petals*
    - Pulse
    - Fumitory
    - Mallow
    - Camelia
    - Ebony
    - Heath
  - *Less Stamens than Petals*
    - Sage or Mint
    - Vervain
    - Broom-rape
    - Bignonia
    - Figwort
    - Olive
    - Jessamine
  - *Sta. and Petals the same*
    - Leadwort
    - Primrose
    - Heath
    - Milkweed
    - Dogbane
    - Holly
    - Sage or Mint
    - Burrage
    - Waterleaf
    - Gentian
    - Plantain
    - Figwort
    - Nightshade
    - Convolvulus
    - Polywonium

Here we are to decide whether the corolla is on the seed-cradle or *below* the seed-cradle. We find that the corolla is below the seed-cradle.

Again we ask the way along the road. Are there more stamens than pistils, fewer stamens than pistils, or are stamens and pistils of the same number?

"Same number!" echoed Harry, wide awake to our new kind of flower lesson.

"Yes; then our flower belongs to some one of the families in the list opposite 'Stamens and pistils the same.' Now listen and I will read to you from this big Botany the descriptions of two or three families and you shall guess to which the flower belongs."

"Here is the description of the Water Leaf family. 'Regular flowers, five-lobed, five stamens, compound, toothed leaves.—"

"No'm, no'm! It isn't a Water Leaf."

"No; well, we will try again. How will this description of the Gentian Family suit our flower? 'Smooth herbs with bitter juice. Leaves opposite, sessile, and entire. Flowers large and handsome.'"

"Flowers large and handsome spoils that," said Allie ruefully. "And I almost thought that description was going to be the one."

"Never mind, Allie; listen again: Burrage Family - sweet-smelling but not square-skinned. Herbs. Alternate leaves. Regular flowers in fives. Flowers in one-sided groups, coiled up at the tip and unfolding slowly as the flowers expand."

"That's just it! That's just it!" cried Allie, jumping from her chair in her delight.

"Yes, this does belong to the Burrage Family. There are several members of this family: and if the afternoon were not so nearly gone, I would read the description of a few of them that you might guess as you have on the 'Family.' But it is so late, we will name our flower at once. Scorpion Grass, or the prettier name, Forget-me-not."

FORGET-ME-NOT.

# LEGEND OF FORGET-ME-NOT.

It was in the golden morning of the early world when an angel sat weeping outside the closed gates of Paradise. He had fallen from his high rank because he had loved a daughter of the earth, nor was he to be allowed to enter Paradise again until this daughter whom he loved had planted the Forget-me-not in every corner of the world. He came down to assist her; and, hand-in-hand, they wandered over the land, planting everywhere the forget-me-not. When their task was ended, then they were allowed both to enter Paradise.

For the beautiful girl, without tasting the bitterness of death, became immortal like the angel whose love she had won as she sat by the riverside twining the Forget-me-nots.

---

### THE FORGET-ME-NOT.

When to the flowers so beautiful,
    The Father gave a name,
Back came a little blue-eyed one,
    All timidly it came.
And standing at its father's feet,
    And gazing in his face,
It said in low and trembling tones,
    And with a modest grace,
"Dear God, the name thou gavest me,
    Alas, I have forgot."
The Father kindly looked him down,
    And said, "Forget-me-not."

---

## MY LADY CLOVER.

Though the brown bee's a rover,
    Seeking ever for sweetness new,
To the little Lady Clover
    He in his heart of hearts is true.
"Sweet! Sweet! Sweet! Sweet!"
    He hums it over and over.
"Where in the wide world will you meet
    With the likes of my Lady Clover?
Pink she is, white she is,
A little thing of delight she is,
Sweet! Sweet! Sweet! Sweet!"
    He hums as he sways above her.
"Nowhere at all do I ever meet
    With the like of my Lady Clover."
"Hollylocks bloom in splendor,
    Red and gold, by the garden wall;
Roses with faces tender;
    Saintly lilies, stately and tall;
But these, these, these
    Pass as the seasons pass;
They care not at all for bees,
    While my clover down in the grass
Is sweet, sweet, sweet, sweet,
    Smiling up at her lover.

"Where in the wild world will you meet
    The truth of my Lady Clover?
Pink she is, white she is,
Sweet as the cheerful light she is.
I come, come, come, come
    From roaming the wide world over."
Sings the bee with a happy hum,
    "Back to my Lady Clover."

———————————

# Our Analysis Chart. - II.

Such fun as we had with our chart from day to day. Hardly one of us but borrowed from our big sisters or brothers, or brought out from the top shelf of our book-cases, some old, forgotten Botany. Hardly any two of us had Botanies alike; but that made no difference. The chart we all had in common, and so we needed the Botany only for "Family" description.

We soon learned that if the plant in question was an *Endogen*, we had only to decide whether it was spadix-like, husk-like, or petal-like, to trace it at once to its family.

Or if the plant in question was an Exogen, we were first to decide whether it was Apetalous, Monopetalous, or Polypetalous. If Apetalous, were the buds in catkins, or not in catkins; if Monopetalous, was the corolla *on* or *below* the seed-cradle; if Polypetalous.

If were the stamens *more* than ten, or *less* than ten. As Harry said, it was like going on a journey into an unknown country, with here and there guide-posts to tell the way. And the guide-posts always told the truth, leading us rightly every time, if only we followed closely what they told us.

# THE LITTLE PINE TREE.

ONCE a little Pine tree,
    In the forest ways,
Sadly sighed and murmured,
    Through the summer days.
"I am clad in needles -
Hateful things!" he cried;
"All the trees about me
    Laugh in scornful pride.
Broad their leaves and fair to see;
Worthless needles cover me."
"Ah! could I have chosen,
    Then, instead of these,
Shining leaves should crown me,
    Shaming all the trees.
Broad as theirs and brighter,
    Dazzling to behold;
All of gleaming silver -
    Nay, of burnished gold.
Then the rest would weep and sigh
None would be so fine as I."

Slept the little Pine tree
    When the night came down,
While the leaves he wished for
    Budded on his crown,
All the forest wondered,
    At the dawn, to see
What a golden fortune
    Decked this little tree.
Then he sang and laughed aloud;
Glad was he and very proud.

Foolish little Pine tree!
    At the close of day,
Through the gloomy twilight,
    Came a thief that way.
Soon the treasure vanished;
    Sighed the Pine, "Alas!
Would that I had chosen

Leaves of crystal glass."
Long and bitterly he wept,
But with night again he slept.

Gladly in the dawning
    Did he wake to find,
That the gentle fairies
    Had again been kind.
How his blazing crystals
    Lit the morning air!
Never had the forest
    Seen a sight so fair.
Then a driving storm did pass;
All his leaves were shattered glass.

Humbly said the Pine tree,
    "I have learned 'tis best
Not to wish for fortunes
    Fairer than the rest.
Glad were I, and thankful,
    If I might be seen,
Like the trees about me,
    Clad in tender green."
Once again he slumbered, sad;
Once again his wish he had.

Broad his leaves and fragrant,
    Rich were they and fine,
Till a goat at noon-day,
    Halted there to dine.
Then her kids came skipping
    Round the fated tree
All his leaves could scarcely
    Make a meal for three.
Every tender bud was nipped,
Every branch and twig was stripped.

Then the wretched Pine tree
    Cried in deep despair,
"Would I had my needles:
    They were green and fair.
Never would I change them,"

Sighed the little tree.
"Just as nature gave them,
    They were the best for me."
So he slept, and waked, and found
All his needles safe and sound.

- EUDORA S. BUMSTEAD, in *St. Nicholas*

---

# Cardinal Flower and Ladies' Tresses

ONE beautiful, hazy, autumn afternoon, we all went flower gathering. Someone had told us that the Lobelias were blossoming in Old Farmer Gray's meadow, and away we flew to find them. Sure enough! there they were in all their rich glory.

While we were gathering the Lobelia, we came upon an odd little plant with white flowers, and such rusty, round, red leaves! They glistened in the sunlight like frost. Very carefully we placed them in our baskets, and then went to search for "Ladies' Tresses," which we were told grew in abundance on the edge of the meadow. In the same field we found some pale, delicate, blue flowers on tall stems, which Allie thought were enough like the Lobelia to be a cousin, at least. Then we found three kinds of yellow flowers and great bunches of Jewel Weed. We were as rich when we turned back home at sunset, as if we had baskets of gold.

Our lesson began the next day with the splendid, scarlet Lobelias - Cardinal Flowers we call them. We noted

CARDINAL FLOWER.

LORELIA.

that the leaves were alternate *without* stipules; that the monopetalous corollas were irregular, *split down one side*; that the five stamens were united by their anthers, and that the one style had an odd-looking stigma, surrounded by fringe; that the stem was simple and smooth; that the leaves were oblong, slightly toothed, sessile, and *sharp at both* ends; that the flowers had bracts, and were gathered in a one-sided raceme at the end of the simple stem.

"This Lobelia, you see, is a rich red; but all the other common Lobelias are blue or purple."

"Then, perhaps these blue flowers I gathered yesterday *are* Lobelias," cried Allie. "I thought they might be."

"You were quite right, Allie; there is no mistaking a Lobelia when once you have learned its characteristics. This one you have is called the Lobelia Inflata because its little capsules are puffed out. And here is another kind, branching and covered with hairs; the flowers are in the axils, and the corolla is small and a pale blue. This specimen is commonly called Indian Tobacco."

"And I see you have two kinds of Jewel Weed, also. What difference do you see, Ned?"

"Some of them are orange-colored with brown spots, and the others are a light yellow."

"Yes, and the leaves are different, too. Those of the dark flowers are almost diamond-shaped, while those of the yellow flowers are oblong, or rather ovate. The Jewel Weed is a sister of the Balsam that we cultivate in the garden. You remember the funny little pods that snap like a little torpedo in your hand, and curl themselves up. The Dodder is especially fond of the Jewel Weed, for some reason or other. You will often find it clinging to its strong branches."

"Of course, you can all tell me at once the family to which these Ladies' Tresses belong."

"They are irregular enough to be Orchids," suggested Lillie Brown, an odd little child who had a way of remembering exact words. "And you told us that when we found

TWIST FLOWER.

a flower like nothing else under the sun, we might reason-
ably expect it would prove to be an Orchid."

"I need to be very careful what I say to Lillie," laughed the
teacher. "She is sure to remember it all *word for word*. And
you are right, Lillie; this is an Orchid - Here is the irregular
gaping perianth of *six pieces*, the outer ones colored, looking like petals. Notice how these Ladies' Tresses, or Twist
Flowers, as they are called in some localities, grow around
the stem or scape. And how fragrant the creamy white flowers are! There is another species of this — smaller flowers
with a yellow lip growing in dense spikes: the stem has
two or three sheaths or bracts and the leaves are narrow
and regularly veined. And a third species, found in damp
shady places, has a stem twisting one way and the flowers
in an opposite way. The scape is tall and slender with two
or three bracts; the leaves grow from the root as these in
the first species, but they are not so slender.

## THE CARDINAL FLOWER.

Have you ever read Longfellow's pretty story of
Hiawatha and Minnehaha?

Well, Indian folk-lore tells us there was another
Hiawatha who had lost his beautiful Minnehaha. This
Hiawatha did not sail off into the sunset to the land of
the hereafter; but very savagely went about the country
shooting with his mighty arrows any beautiful maiden he
chanced to see.

One bright sunny day he lay down by a brook to rest.

So soft were the sun's rays and so gentle the breezes that this angry-hearted Hiawatha was lulled to sleep. It is sad indeed that I cannot tell you that he rose from his refreshing sleep more gently disposed towards the maidens of his own land. But, alas, the beautiful doesn't always prevail even in legends; and the sad truth is that this savage young warrior's first act was to kill a beautiful maiden who chanced to be looking at her bright reflection in the water, and singing to herself as she plaited her shining locks of jet black hair.

And so incensed was Mother Earth, that on that spot where the maiden's heart blood spilled, she sent forth this blood-red cardinal flower.

———

### PUT FLOWERS IN YOUR WINDOW.

Put flowers in your window, friend,
    And summer in your heart;
The greenness of their mimic boughs
    Is of the woods a part;
The color of their tender bloom
    Is love's own pleasing hue,
As surely as you smile on them,
    They'll smile again on you.

Put flowers in your window, when
    You sit in idle mood;
For wholesome, mental ailment,
    There is no cheaper food.
For love and hope and charity
    Are in there censer shrined,
And shapes of loveliest thought grow out
    The flower-loving mind.

———

# NARCISSUS.

One day a youth named Narcissus had been hunting in the forest. He lost sight of his companions, and while looking for them, chanced to see a fountain flashing beneath a stray sunbeam.

He drew near. As he knelt upon the mossy bank, he saw his own image in the water. He thought it some lovely water-sprite that lived within the fountain.

"You are the most beautiful being my eyes ever looked upon," said he, "you shall have all that is mine and I will forever be your faithful friend if you will only come with me."

The image only smiled and poor Narcissus, in the hope of winning so beautiful a companion, hung over the brink of the fountain forgetting his food and rest, but not losing sight for an instant of the lovely face.

Day after day and night after night he stayed there, gazing and grieving. He grew thin and pale and weak, until, worn out with disappointment, he pined away and died.

When his friends found poor dead Narcissus, they were filled with sorrow, and went about sadly to prepare a funeral pile. But, most wonderful to tell! When they returned to bear away the body, it could nowhere be found, and before their astonished eyes, a little flower rose from the water's edge, just where their friend had died.

They named the flower in memory of him, and it has been called Narcissus unto this very day.

- ST. NICHOLAS.

CATKIN OF THE OAK.

# Trees of History and Mythology.

A YOUTH once rode into a forest, and asked of the trees:
    "O, if ye have a singing leaf,
        I pray you give it me."
But the trees all kept their council,
    They said neither yea or nay:
Only there sighed from the pine tops
    The music of seas far away;
Only the Aspen pattered
    With a sound like the growing rain,

> That fell fast and ever faster,
>     Then faltered to silence again.

Tennyson tells us of the talking Oak, but to us, who are less fortunate in poetic imagery, the trees are speechless; if the birds understand the language of rustling leaves, they keep it a secret from us, who would fain open and read this page in nature's volume.

Sacred history is full of allusions to trees in their various stages of growth and abundance. The first sin of our common mother was in partaking of the forbidden fruit from the tree in the garden of Paradise. At the foot of Mount Lebanon, eight gigantic Cedars stand as the only representatives of the once immense forests. The prophecy concerning them has come to pass, "They shall be few that a child may count them." The Olive, the Fig and the Oak are likewise often referred to in the sacred Scriptures. We read of the righteous as representing a tree of life, and they are declared to be like a tree planted by the rivers of water, while the wicked are likened to a Green Bay tree, and the ungodly to an Oak, whose leaf fadeth. The Green Bay tree is a species of Laurel. Pliny collected and recorded the information and opinions concerning it current in his time. It was held sacred to Apollo, and used as a symbol of victory. It was used by the Romans to guard the gates of Caesar, and that worn by Augustus and his successors had a miraculous history. The grove at the Imperial villa having grown from a shoot sent by Livius Drusilla from heaven.

Among the Indians of Brazil, there is a tradition that the whole human race sprang from a Palm tree. It has been a symbol of excellence for things good and beautiful. Among the ancients, it was an emblem of victory, and, as such, was worn by the early Christian martyrs, and has been found sculptured on their tombs. The Mohammedans venerate it. Certain trees, said to have been propagated from some originally planted by the prophet's daughter, are held sacred and the fruit sold at enormous prices. The day upon which Christ entered Jerusalem, riding upon the colt of an ass, is called Palm Sunday, being the first day of the Holy Week. In Europe, real palm branches are distributed among the people. Goethe says:

> "In Rome on Palm Sunday,
>     They have the true Palms,
> The cardinals bow reverently
>     And sing old psalms."

Elsewhere these songs are sung 'mid Olive branches; more southern climes must be content with the sad Willow.

The books relating to the religion of Buddha were nearly all of them written upon the leaves of the Fan Palm, and by missionaries, they have been used in the place of paper. The noble aspect of this tree, together with its surpassing utility, has caused it to be called "the prince of the vegetable kingdom," and it has been immortalized in history, mythology and poetry.

A Cypress tree in Somma, Lombardy, is said to have been standing since the time of Julius Caesar. Napoleon, in making a road over the Simplon, deviated from a straight

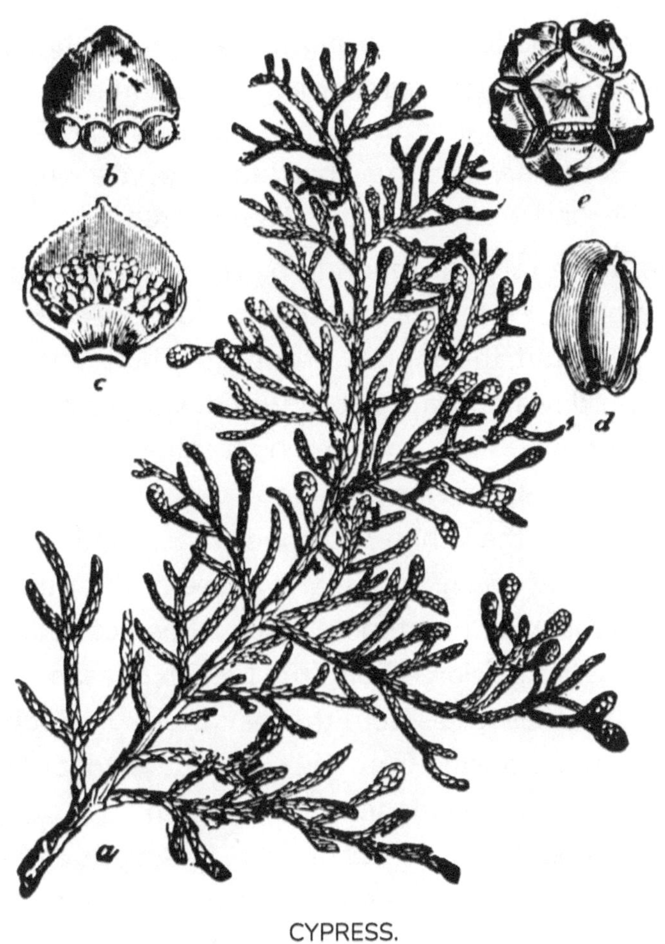

CYPRESS.

line, that he might not be obliged to cut it down. Cypress wood is very enduring, and for this reason, no doubt, it was used for mummy cases and statues. Pliny tells us a statue of Jupiter carved from Cypress wood remained standing for six hundred years. In Turkish cemeteries, it is a rule to plant a tree of this variety at every interment.

Cypanissus, a beautiful youth, was transformed into a

Cypress by Apollo, that he might grieve all the time. The Cypress is an emblem of mourning, and Scott thus writes:

"When villagers my shroud bestrew with Pansies, Rosemary, and Rue, then lady, weave a wreath for me, and weave it of the Cypress tree."

There is a familiar legend about the Black Thorn, a species of the Plum. It is said that Joseph, of Aramathea, planted his staff, that it grew, put forth its blossoms every Christmas day afterward until it was destroyed by a Puritan soldier, who was wounded by a splint from the tree and died from its effects.

Branches of the White Thorn were used for the nuptial chaplets of Athenian brides, and a tree of this variety is still alive that was planted by Mary, Queen of Scots.

There is a tradition among the French peasantry that groans and cries issue from the Hawthorn on Good Friday, doubtless, arising from the superstition that Christ's crown of thorns was made from this bush.

The legend that the cross of Jesus was made of Aspen wood, and hence its leaves were doomed to tremble, has led an unknown poet to show his ignorance of the true cause in the following lines:

"Ah, tremble, tremble, Aspen tree,
I need not ask thee why thou shakest,
For if, as holy legend saith,
On thee the Saviour bled to death,
No wonder, Aspen that thou quakest,
And till in judgment all assemble,
Thy leaves, accursed, shall wail and tremble."

The real cause of the mobility depends on the fact

that the leaf stalk of the Poplar is flattened laterally, and even the slightest wind produces a motion. Since this is so, we may be sure that the Aspen will continue to wail and tremble, but not because its leaves are accursed.

BLACKTHORNS.

There is an island in Lake Wetter, Scotland, upon which stood twelve majestic Beech trees, called the twelve apostles. A jealous peasant cut one of them down, thus effacing from the group the traitor, Judas, who, he declared, should have no lot with the faithful.

In Latin myths, the Fig tree was held sacred to Bacchus, and employed in religious ceremonies. A tree of this variety is said to have over-shadowed Romulus and Remus, the twin founders of Rome, in the wolf's cave. The sacred Fig is chiefly planted in India as a religious object, being regarded as sacred by both Brahmas and Buddhists. A gigantic tree of this variety, growing in Ceylon, is said to be one of the oldest trees in the world, and if tradition is to be trusted, it grew from a branch of the tree under which Gantama Buddha became endowed with divine powers, and has always been held in the highest veneration.

- F. L. SHELDON in Vick's Magazine.

## The Christmas Rose.

A LITTLE way up one of the Rhatian Alps, beneath the shade of an old black pine, grew a Christmas rose. The summer had passed, and the short days had come when the wind blows and the snow flies, and the hardy little mountain rose had two buds. "Dear me," fretted the rose, "I wish I could blossom when other plants do. There would be some pleasure in showing one's self to the dainty blue gentian or the pretty eyebright; but with no one to admire me, I see no use in blooming at all."

"Ho! Ho!" laughed the old pine, waving his shaggy arms, - "Ho! Ho! What a little grumbler. The snow and I will admire you. You are named after the blessed Christ-child and ought to be happy and contented. Push up through the deepening snow, little friend, and expand your buds into perfect blossoms; we were all made for a wise purpose, and we shall know what it is when the time comes, if—"

Just then, the north wind blew so hard the old pine was quite out of breath, and for some reason, he never renewed the conversation.

"All the world is dead except the pine and me," murmured the rose. "Perhaps I had better follow his advice. If I was made for a wise purpose, I shall not be forgotten." So she took good care of her beautiful buds, and the day before Christmas, the black pine saw her blossoms, white and perfect, peering up through the white snow.

Now the two little children of Klotz, the woodcutter, were nearly heartbroken; for their mother was sick, and that morning, the kind neighbor who had watched by her side through the night said, "God pity this home; I fear your mother will die before night." Their father sat by the fireplace, speechless with grief, and answered them neither by word nor look when they crept up to him for comfort. So at last, they stole out of the door, and, hand in hand, wandered a short way up the mountainside, following the forester's tracks till they came in sight of the old black pine.

"If all the mothers in the world were dying, that hard old pine would not care!" said the boy bitterly. "Let us go back into the valley, sister; there we shall find good people with kind hearts, while there is no one to care for us here."

"There is one who cares for us even here," cried the sister, spying the Christmas roses, and in a moment, she had scraped away the snow and plucked them. "We had forgotten the Christ-child, and that tomorrow is His birth-day. Let us take the roses to the church and there pray that our mother's life may be spared."

So they hastened down the mountain to the village church, where they found the good pastor busy trimming the altar for the Christmas festival. He took the flowers and put them with some feathery moss into a tall white vase. Then he knelt with the children and prayed for their mother's life, and the roses, nodding on their stems, smiled as though the gift asked for were already granted. When they returned home, their father met them at the door and exclaimed joyfully, "The fever has turned, and your mother is better. Thank God!"

The Christmas rose had fulfilled its destiny, for it had inspired hope in the minds and gladdened the hearts of the poor little children. We were all made for a wise purpose, and we shall learn what it is in God's own good time.

> The fields with daisies are besprent
>   As white as flakes of snow,
> And from the whispering woods are sent
> Joy-murmurs soft and low.
>
> The tiny brook, that lay in trance

Beneath the North King's spell,
Once more upon its way doth dance,
Its happiness to tell,
And with a kindly touch to lend
A little timely aid
To many a dear half-famished friend
In valley and in glade.

- AMERICAN GARDEN.

## St. John's wort – Foxglove – Loosestrife – Drosera or Sundew.

WHEN we first began to study botany, we were very much inclined to look upon the common flowers as quite beneath our notice. Indeed, one of the boys, a rather coarse lad, who had had very little in his life to help him be very much of a gentleman, had pulled up a plant by the root and tossed it over into an adjoining field, saying with a sneer, "What's that weed good for?"

But we all learned a lesson that day that we never forgot, for our teacher picked up the despised weed, brought it to us, and showed us such a wonderful arrangement of its petals and stamens and told us such a beautiful old-time legend about it. We never forgot the lesson; and so, when the same boy brought in a big branch of the common St. John's wort to the schoolroom one day, we were ready to accept from it any wonderful secret it might see fit to disclose.

"Edward has brought the plant that the early Church dedicated to John the Baptist — the St. John's wort. I hope,

ST. JOHN'SWORT.

Edward, you gathered this plant when the sun was in the sky, for the old English myth regarding this plant tells us that if we gather it, or step on it, or in any way trouble it after sunset, a fairy horse will spring up at our feet and carry us off over hill and dale, leaving us just where the sunrise finds us. And as the fairy horses are very swift, there is no telling where we might find ourselves after such a fearful gallop.

"I didn't think it was worth bringing at first," said Edward; "but the more I looked at it, the more I saw in it. The stamens are in different clusters, and the flowers are covered over with black specks — they look as if they were mildewed. And the leaves are singular too. They seemed full of holes, but as I held them up to the light, I found they were not holes — only thin places."

"Those are the distinguishing characteristics of the St. John's wort, Edward. And there are about thirty kinds of St. John's wort in this country — some of them very delicate and pretty.

"And here are some Foxgloves — the very largest species of the wild Foxglove. See its bell-shaped calyx, the

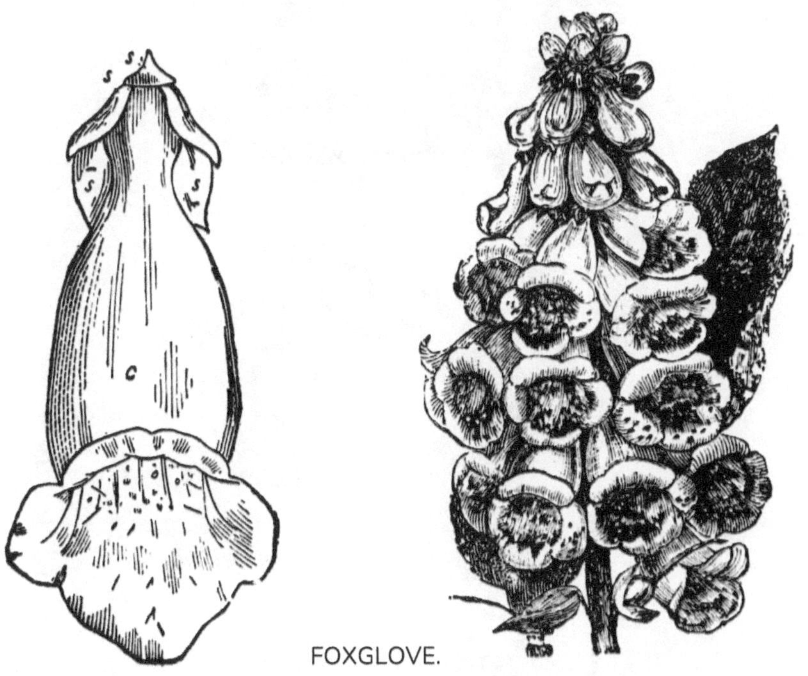

FOXGLOVE.

puffed-out corolla; these four woolly stamens! And this one, dried and gone to seed, shows us the ovate capsule with its partition of the many seeds packed away in the little compartments — a real storehouse, you see, for next year's use. Notice that the lower leaves are opposite, while the upper ones are alternate. Purple stems covered

YELLOW LOOSESTRIFE.

with a whitish powder. What a pretty spike these yellow trumpet-shaped blossoms make! No wonder it was chosen as one of the Fairy Flowers. It was said that when the foxes attended the Fairy dances, they always put on the flowers for gloves."

"Lillie, what is that whorl-leaved plant you have? Describe it to the class."

"The leaves are narrow, in whorls of threes, fours, or fives. There is one blossom in the axil of every leaf, and these blossoms have five stamens with purple anthers. The corolla is streaked with purple, and the leaves are spotted, something like the St. John's wort."

FOUR-LEAVED LOOSESTRIFE.

"It is the Loose-strife, Lillie, I am sure. There is one kind out on the prairies that is very beautiful. It has a slender, four-angled stem, branches with stiff, shiny leaves without dots. Its large, brilliant yellow flowers make it one of the most beautiful sights on the prairies.

The little, common yellow flower-myrtle is a Loose-strife too. That, as you all know, has a trailing stem with pretty little round leaves on very short stems. The yellow blossoms are in the axils, they, too, very close-sitting.

And now, last but not least, Allie brings us a curious little plant with white flowers and round leaves covered over with little hairs, every one of which is tipped with a bright shining point that glistens like dew. Everything about the blossom is in fives, and the scape is coiled up at the top as the ferns are coiled when they are not yet grown. The most singular feature of this little Drosera or Sundew is its *divided stigmas* — it looks as if there were just double the number of stigmas that really are.

---

### DIMPLE AND ROSY-WING.

Under the daisies two little fairies,
    Dimple and Rosy-wing,
Across a stem of red strawberries
    Made a grass-blade tilt and swing.

"Ho!" said Dimple, "now for a ride."
"Now for a tilt," said both together.
One on each end they jumped astride,
    And up went Dimple, light as a feather;

And down in the grass went Rosy-wing;
    But he kicked with his dainty feet,

And up he went with a flutter and spring,
    Up where the daisies and grass-heads meet.

Up and down they balanced and swung,
    And laughed so loud, the bumblebees
Turned on the clovers where they hung,
    And stared and rubbed their dusty knees.

A grasshopper, walking up a daisy,
    Cheered and cheered; and a cricket frisked
Out of his hole, as if he were crazy,
    Cackled and laughed, and back he whisked.

By – and - by, at the close of day,
    Their mother came; and when they told her,
She kissed them, and gayly bore them away,
    Dancing off with one on each shoulder.

- BY ANNETTE BISHOP.

---

# A Sermon from a Thorn-apple Tree.

I WANT to tell you about my Thorn-apple Tree. It came up by the gate where it gets the drip from the watering-trough — that's what made it grow so strong and handsome. Every year it is just as full of blossoms as the apple trees, and you know what it bears — little, red, seedy berries, good for nothing at all, so I used to think.

But the first spring after I was sick, when I was thinking how pretty it was — all blown out, and the green leaves peeping through the white — it just came to me that the Thorn-apple was doing what it was made for exactly, the same as the russet trees and the pippins; and I took notice, as I never did before, how the squirrels came to eat the seeds in the fall, and how the blue jays and the winter-birds seemed always to find something there for breakfast, and I came to love that Thorn-apple, and enjoy it more than anything else.

It always seemed to have some lesson for me. I call it my preacher, and whenever I look at it, I think the Lord wants Thorn-apples as well as pippins. He sets a good many of His children to feeding birds and squirrels and doing little things that nobody takes any note of, and I'm thankful every day that He lets me grow the blossoms and feed His birds.

Perhaps that is all He may want of you, Ruby, but don't you be troubled about that. 'Abide in Him,' as the branch abideth in the vine, and He'll see to the fruit. It will be just the kind He wants you to bear."

- FROM EMILY HUNTINGTON MILLER'S "Thorn-Apple."

---

### THE PETRIFIED FERN.

IN a valley, centuries ago,
Grew a little Fern leaf, green and slender;
Veining delicate and fibers tender;
Waving, when the wind crept down so low.
Rushes tall and moss and grass grew round it,
Playful sunbeams darted in and found it,
Drops of dew stole in by night and crowned it,
But no foot of man e'er trod that way.
Earth was young and keeping holiday.

Monster fishes swam the silent main,
Stately forests waved their giant branches,
Mountains hurled their snowy avalanches,

Mammoth creatures stalked across the plain;
Nature reveled in grand mysteries,
But the little Fern was not of these,
Did not number with the hills and trees;
Only grew and waved its wild, sweet way;
No one came to note it day by day.

Earth one time put on a frolic mood,
Heaved the rocks and changed the mighty motion
Of the deep, strong currents of the ocean,
Moved the plain and shook the haughty wood,
Crushed the little Fern in soft, moist clay,
Covered it and hid it safe away.
Oh, the long, long centuries since that day!
Oh, the changes, oh, life's bitter cost,
Since that useless little Fern was lost!

Useless? Lost? There came a thoughtful man
Searching nature's secrets far and deep;
From a fissure in a rocky steep
He withdrew a stone o'er which there ran
Fairy pencilings, a quaint design,
Veinings, leafage, fibers clear and fine,
And the Fern's life lay in every line.
So, I think, God hides some souls away,
Sweetly to surprise us the last day.

- MARY L. BOLLES BRANCH

---

# Gerardias – Chickweed – Pimpernel – Mullein – Evening Primrose.

"REAL Gerardias?" exclaimed our teacher, one day, as Allie hurried to meet her with her hands full of beautiful purple flowers. "I haven't seen a Gerardia for years. Where did you find them, Allie?

"I am always so glad that flowers are the same year after year! Here is the same short-tubed calyx with its little fine teeth; the same long-tubed corolla: the meandering, branching stem with the narrow, rough-edged leaves."

"A little later you will, I think, find another species of the Gerardia, smaller than this and very pretty. Its purple corolla you will find spotted within and the flower, not so close-sitting as this, growing from the axils of the leaves. These two are the only Gerardias we have in the Northern States."

"And Ned has some Chickweed!"

"I was going to carry that home to my bird," answered Ned. "I didn't bring it for the Botany class."

"You didn't think it worth our time, I suppose; but there may be more to it than you think. Nothing do we need in this world, Ned, so much as to get it fixed in our minds that we should sneer at nothing. As we grow older, if we are thoughtful and wide-awake, we shall be continually learning that when we see nothing in things, the fault is, nine times out of ten, in us — not in the thing."

"This little starry-eyed Chickweed is good for the birds, to be sure; but it is also good for us. Lord Bacon, one of the greatest thinkers and writers the world has ever known, thought it worth while to study the little Chick-weed thoroughly, and then to write about it. In England, the Chickweed is called 'The Poor Man's Barometer.' And a very reliable barometer it is, too; for, as Lord Bacon wrote, 'When the flower expands boldly and fully in the morning, no rain will happen for four hours or more. If it continues

GERARDIA.

49

open, no rain will disturb the summer day. When it *half* conceals its miniature flower, the day is generally showery; but if it entirely shuts up, or veils the white flower with its green mantle, let the traveler put on his greatcoat, and the ploughman expect rest from his labor.'"

There is another little flower, too, that makes a very pretty sort of barometer, and is as noted for foretelling the weather as the little Chickweed or Stellaria Media.

CHICKWEED.

# PIMPERNEL OR SHEPHERD'S CLOCK.

When the weather is fine, the scarlet petals open regularly between seven and eight in the morning, and close at two in the afternoon; but if damp and cloudy, they will not open at all. It is so constant in its hours that it has sometimes been called the *Shepherd's Clock*. One writer says of it -

> "I'll go and look at the Pimpernel,
> And see if she thinks the clouds look well!
> > For if the sun shine,
> > And 'tis like to be fine,
> > I will go to the fair!
> So, Pimpernel, what bode the clouds in the sky?
> If fair weather, no maiden so merry as I!"
>
> Now the Pimpernel flower had folded up
> Her little gold star in her coral cup,
> > And unto the maid
> > A warning she said:
> > "Though the sun smite down,
> > There's a gathering frown
> O'er the checkered blue of the clouded sky;
> So, tarry at home for a storm is nigh."

"Tell me about your flower, Harry. It is what children call 'Butter and Eggs,' isn't it?"

"Yes, and if we squeeze the sides of the flower it will open and shut its mouth. Sometimes we call it Horse's Lip."

"And we must learn another name for it, now that we are growing so wise. We must call it Toad-flax, from the resemblance of its leaves to the common flax. Here are three kinds of Toad-flax. If you look at the base of the stem,

PIMPERNEL.

MULLEIN.

near the roots of this little blue-spurred Toad-flax, you will find one or two little shoots with roundish, opposite or whorled leaves, different from the leaves on the main stalk. These little shoots are the distinguishing features of this species.

The Toad-flax that you call 'Butter and Eggs' is the Common Toad-flax; the third kind is this little creeping plant with ear-shaped leaves, the yellow corolla with a bright purple upper lip. This kind is often named to children as 'Three Birds' because some fanciful flower lovers have thought the odd-shaped corolla resembled three tiny birds sitting on the spur."

"And now have we examined all our flowers?" asked our teacher, looking about the room.

"All but this elegant Mullein-stalk," answered Harry, a mischievous twinkle in his eye.

"I don't see what this honest old Quaker has done to be slighted by you, Harry! Now, I rather like him with his clean, drab woolly suit, and his stiff, upright habits. He stands like a gray-bearded sentinel by the wayside, and you should address him respectfully as 'Friend Verbascum' — for that is his name."

"And is the pretty little Moth Mullein a relative of his?" asked Allie.

"Yes, she is none other than his own sister Blattaria, although she considers a green robe more becoming to her beauty than drab. She inherits quite a little of the family stiffness, but on the whole you will find her a very interesting person if you will take the pains to make her

EVENING PRIMROSE.

acquaintance. She wears yellow flowers with brown backs. The stamens of the flowers are of unequal length and are covered with brilliant purple hairs. Her leaves are deep green, notched and smooth, clasping closely about the stem.

There is, too, another member of this family, the White Mullein. He is rather more aristocratic in his tastes. He wears a livery of rich green leaves with drab-white linings, and a coronet of gold-colored flowers. He is found now and then about Lake Oneida, in New York, but for the most part, he spends his time 'abroad.'

And here is the little Evening Primrose; but we shall need to have an evening party if we are to examine these and see them wide awake. They are not all fond of the sun and keep their eyes shut tight through the day. They are military little flowers — that is, they close with a pop just at sunrise; in other words, they fire a salute to announce the approach of the sun, and then close their windows tight and lower the shades until something tells them the great Sun is gone again."

## LITTLE PURPLE ASTER.

Little Purple Aster, sitting on her stem,
Peeping at the passers-by, beckoning at them,
Staring o'er at Golden Rod, by the pasture bars,
Giving him a timid nod when he turns his stars.
Little Purple Aster, waits till very late,
Till the flow'rs have faded from the garden gate,
Then when all is dreary, see her buds unfurled,
Come to cheer a changeful and sombre autumn world.

---

## THE TREE.

The tree's early leaf-buds were bursting their brown.
"Shall I take them away?" said the frost sweeping down.
    "No; leave them alone
    Till the blossoms have grown,"
Prayed the tree, while he trembled from rootlet to crown.

The tree bore his blossoms, and all the birds sung.
"Shall I take them away?" said the wind as he swung.
    "No; leave them alone
    Till the berries have grown,"
Said the tree, while his leaflets quivering hung.

The tree bore his fruit in the midsummer glow.
Said the child, "May I gather thy berries now?"
    "Yes; all thou canst see;
    Take them; all are for thee,"
Said the tree, while he bent down his laden boughs low.

—BJORNSTJERNE BJORNSON

# The Last Dream of the Old Oak Tree.

## A CHRISTMAS TALE.

IN the forest, high up on the steep shore, hard by the open sea-coast, stood a very old oak tree. It was exactly three hundred and sixty-five years old, but that long time was not more for the tree than just as many days would be to us men. We wake by day and sleep through the night, and then we have our dreams; it is different with the tree, which keeps awake through three seasons of the year, and does not get its sleep till winter comes. Winter is its time for rest, its night after the long day which is called spring, summer, and autumn.

On many a warm summer day, the ephemera, the fly that lives but for a day, had danced around his crown — had lived, enjoyed, and felt happy; and then rested for a moment in quiet bliss — the tiny creature — on one of the great fresh oak leaves; and then the tree always said:

"Poor little thing! Your whole life is but a single day. How very short! It's quite melancholy!"

"Melancholy? Why do you say that?" the ephemera would then always reply. "It is wonderfully bright, warm, and beautiful all around me, and that makes me rejoice!"

"But only one day and then it's all done!"

"Done?" repeated the ephemera. "What's the meaning of *done*? Are you done too?"

"No; I shall live perhaps thousands of your days, and my day is whole seasons long! It's something so long that you can't at all manage to reckon it out."

"No? Then I don't understand you. You say you have thousands of my days; but I have thousands of moments, in which I can be merry and happy. Does all the beauty of this world cease when you die?"

"No," replied the tree, "it will certainly last much longer — far longer than I can possibly think."

"Well, then, we have the same time, only that we reckon differently."

And the ephemera danced and floated in the air, and rejoiced in her delicate wings of gauze and velvet, and rejoiced in the balmy breezes laden with the fragrance of meadows and of wild roses and elder flowers; of the garden hedges, wild thyme, and mint, and daisies; the scent of these was all so strong that the ephemera was almost intoxicated. The day was long and beautiful, full of joy and of sweet feeling, and when the sun sank low, the little fly felt very agreeably tired of all its happiness and enjoyment. The delicate wings would not carry it anymore, and quietly and slowly it glided down upon the soft grass-blade, nodded its head as well as it could nod, and went quietly to sleep — and was dead.

"Poor little ephemera!" said the oak. "That was a terribly short life!"

And on every summer day, the same dance was

repeated, the same question and answer, and the same sleep. The same thing was repeated through whole generations of ephemera, all of them felt equally merry and equally happy.

The oak stood there awake through the spring morning, the noon of summer, and the evening of autumn; and its time of rest, its night, was coming on apace. Winter was approaching.

Already the storms were singing their "good-night, good-night!" Here fell a leaf and there fell a leaf.

"We'll rock you and dandle you! Go to sleep, go to sleep! We sing you to sleep, we shake you to sleep, but it does you good in your old twigs, does it not? They seem to crack for very joy! Sleep sweetly, sleep sweetly! It's your three hundred and sixty-fifth night. Properly speaking, you're only a stripling as yet. Sleep sweetly! The clouds strew down snow, there will be quite a coverlet, warm and protecting, around your feet. Sweet sleep to you, and pleasant dreams!"

And the oak tree stood there denuded of all its leaves, to sleep through the long winter, and to dream many a dream, always about something that had happened to it — just as in the dreams of men.

The great oak had once been small — indeed, an acorn had been its cradle. According to human computation, it was now in its fourth century. It was the greatest and best tree in the forest; its crown towered far above all the other trees, and could be descried from afar across the sea, so that it served as a landmark to the sailors: the tree had no idea how many eyes were in the habit of seeking it. High up in its green summit the wood-pigeon built her nest, and the cuckoo sat in its boughs, and sang his song; and in autumn, when the leaves looked like thin plates of copper, the birds of passage came and rested there, before they flew away across the sea; but now it was winter, and the tree stood there leafless, so that everyone could see how gnarled and crooked the branches were that shot forth from its trunk. Crows and rooks came and took their seats by turns in the boughs, and spoke of the hard times which were beginning, and of the difficulty of getting a living in winter.

It was just at the holy Christmas time, when the tree dreamed its most glorious dream.

The tree had a distinct feeling of the festive time and fancied he heard the bells ringing from the churches all around; and yet it seemed as if it were a fine summer's day, mild and warm. Fresh and green, he spread out his mighty crown; the sunbeams played among the twigs and the leaves; the air was full of the fragrance of herbs and blossoms; gay butterflies chased each other to and fro. The ephemeral insects danced as if all the world were created merely for them to dance and be merry in. All that the tree had experienced for years and years, and that had happened around him, seemed to pass by him again, as in a festive pageant. He saw the knights of ancient days ride by with their noble dames on gallant steeds, with plumes waving in their bonnets and falcons on their wrists. The hunting horn sounded, and the dogs barked.

He saw hostile warriors in colored jerkins and with shining weapons, with spear and halberd, pitching their tents and striking them again. The watch fires flamed up anew, and men sang and slept under the branches of the tree. He saw loving couples meeting near his trunk, happily, in the moonshine; and they cut the initials of their names in the gray-green bark of his stem. Once — but long years had rolled by since then — zitherns and Æolian harps had been hung up on his boughs by merry wanderers; and now they hung there again, and once again they sounded in tones of marvelous sweetness. The wood pigeons cooed as if they were telling what the tree felt in all this, and the cuckoo called out to tell him how many summer days he had yet to live.

Then it appeared to him as if new life were rippling down into the remotest fiber of his root and mounting up into his highest branches, to the tops of the leaves. The tree felt that he was stretching and spreading himself, and through his root, he felt that there was new life and motion even in the ground itself. He felt his strength increase, he grew higher, his stem shot up unceasingly, and he grew more and more; his crown became fuller, and spread out; and in proportion as the tree grew, he felt his happiness increase, and his joyous hope that he should reach even higher — quite up to the warm, brilliant sun.

Already had he grown high above the clouds, which floated past beneath his crown like dark troops of passage birds, or like great white swans. And every leaf of the tree had the gift of sight, as if it had eyes wherewith to see. The stars became visible in broad daylight, great and sparkling; each of them sparkled like a pair of eyes, mild and clear. They recalled to his memory well-known gentle eyes, eyes of children, eyes of lovers who had met beneath his boughs.

It was a marvelous spectacle, and one full of happiness and joy. And yet amid all this happiness, the tree felt a longing, a yearning desire that all other trees of the wood beneath him, and all the bushes and herbs and flowers, might be able to rise with him, that they too might see this splendor, and experience this joy. The great majestic oak was not quite happy in his happiness while he had not them all, great and little, about him; and this feeling of yearning trembled through his every twig, through his every leaf, warmly and fervently as through a human heart.

The crown of the tree waved to and fro, as if he sought something in his silent longing, and he looked down. Then he felt the fragrance of thyme, and soon afterward, the more powerful scent of honeysuckle and violets; and he fancied he heard the cuckoo answering him.

Yes, through the clouds, the green summits of the forest came peering up, and under himself, the oak saw the other trees, as they grew and raised themselves aloft. Bushes and herbs shot up high, and some tore themselves up bodily by the roots to rise the quicker. The birch was the quickest of all. Like a white streak of lightning, its slender stem shot upwards in a zigzag line, and the branches spread around it like green gauze and like banners; the whole woodland natives, even to the brown-plumed rushes, grew up with the rest, and the birds came too, and sang; and on the grass blade that fluttered aloft like a long silken ribbon into the air, sat the grasshopper cleaning his wings with his legs; the May beetles hummed, and the bees murmured, and every bird sang in his appointed manner; all was song and sound of gladness up into the high heaven.

"But the little blue flower by the water side, where is that?" said the oak; "and the purple bell-flower and the daisy?" For, you see, the old oak tree wanted to have them all about him.

"We are here — we are here!" was shouted and sung in reply.

"But the beautiful thyme of last summer — and in the last year there was certainly a place here covered with lilies of the valley! And the wild apple tree that blossomed so splendidly! And all the glory of the wood that came year by year — if that had only just been born, it might have been here now!"

"We are here, we are here!" replied voices still higher in the air. It seemed as if they had flown on before.

"Why, that is beautiful, indescribably beautiful!" exclaimed the old oak tree, rejoicingly. "I have them all around me, great and small—not one has been forgotten! How can so much happiness be imagined? How can it be possible?"

"In heaven, in the better land, it can be imagined, and it is possible!" the reply sounded through the air.

And the old tree, who grew on and on, felt how his roots were tearing themselves free from the ground.

"That's right, that's better than all!" said the tree. "Now, no fetters hold me! I can fly up now, to the very highest, in glory and in light. And all my beloved ones are with me, great and small — all of them, all!"

That was the dream of the old oak tree; and while he dreamt thus, a mighty storm came rushing over land and sea — at the holy Christmas-tide. The sea rolled great billows toward the shore; there was a crackling and crashing in the tree — his root was torn out of the ground in the very moment while he was dreaming that his root freed itself from the earth. He fell. His three hundred and sixty-five years were now as the single day of the ephemera.

On the morning of the Christmas festival, when the sun rose, the storm had subsided. From all the churches sounded the festive bells, and from every hearth, even from the smallest hut, arose the smoke in blue clouds, like the smoke from the altars of the Druids of old at the feast of thanks-offerings. The sea became gradually calm, and on board a great ship in the offing, that had fought successfully with the tempest, all the flags were displayed, as a token of joy suitable to the festive day.

"The tree is down — the old oak tree, our landmark on the coast!" said the sailors. "It fell in the storm of last night. Who can replace it? No one can."

This was the funeral oration — short, but well meant — that was given to the tree, which lay stretched on the snowy covering on the sea-shore; and over its prostrate form sounded the notes of a song from the ship, a carol of the joys of Christmas, and of the redemption of the soul of man by His blood, and of eternal life.

> "Sing, sing aloud, this blessed morn —
> It is fulfilled — and He is born:
> Oh, joy without compare!
> Hallelujah! Hallelujah!"

Thus sounded the old psalm-tune, and everyone on board the ship felt lifted up in his own way through the song and the prayer, just as the old tree had felt lifted up in its last, its most beauteous dream in the Christmas night.

— HANS CHRISTIAN ANDERSEN

---

Friendship is a sheltering tree.

— COLERIDGE, Youth and Age

---

> Pray, where are the charming bluebells gone,
>     That lately bloomed in the wood?
> Why, the little fairies have each taken one,
>     And put it on for a hood.
>
> And where are the pretty grass-stalks gone,
>     That waved in the summer breeze?
> Oh, the fairies have taken them every one,
>     To plant in their gardens like trees.

# Grass of Parnassus. - Mimulus. - Flower of Circe.

"EVERYONE should know the Grass of Parnassus," said our teacher at the opening of our next lesson. "One or another of its beautiful kinds are to be found along the streamlets all over the United States. It is a white flower, opening like a star, in early autumn. It has, as you see, five white petals, marked very delicately *with green or purple veins; five sepals united at the base, and two rows of stamens.* The outside stamens are in groups, and each one has a little globe-shaped head in the place of the usual anther; so, after all, the inner row are the true stamens. And such a smooth plant, with heart-shaped leaves, and scapes with one sessile leaf, and one terminal flower."

"Harry declares this flower looks like a monkey," said Fannie, bringing forward a little blue flower.

"Harry has a wonderful imagination, I know, Fannie; but isn't it strange, other people have thought the very same thing — even some of the great botanists — and have really named it 'Mimulus Oringeus,' which means 'gaping monkey.'"

Harry looked very superior as the teacher said this, and we all laughed at him.

"Describe the flower, Harry, that you so fortunately named," said the teacher.

"I'm afraid I can guess better than I can describe," replied Harry, scowling hard at the little plant. "It has sessile leaves; axillary flowers; leaves rather lance-shaped; calyx a tube, five-toothed; four stamens; a thick stigma; corolla five-parted, irregular, pale blue outside, and yellowish inside. The stem is square."

GRASS OF PARNASSUS.

68

"There is another flower that one of the haymakers showed me, one day in the summer, that looked like a snake's head," said Willie Carroll. "Its mouth was open, and its long tongue was out. It had large white flowers; a five-parted calyx, with little bracts; a two-parted corolla, and five stamens, with funny, wooly anthers. The flowers were in spikes."

"You did well to remember all that, Willie. I'm proud of you. Your description is so true, I know at once that it must have been the Chelone (Tortoise), or, as the country people call it, 'Snake's Head'."

"But here's a flower in Allie's hands that has a story. I know you'll be ready for that. Its name is Enchanter's Nightshade. See the odd, little, prickly capsules on these lower flowers that have already gone to seed. They stick to our clothes like beggar's ticks. The blossoms, you see, have a two-parted calyx; two petals; two stamens, and a two-celled seed-cradle. And the flower is, in botanical language, the Circoea, named from the witch Circe. The witch was celebrated for her knowledge of poisonous herbs. She married the Prince of Colchis and murdered him that she might govern the kingdom herself. Her angry subjects, when they learned what she had done, drove her from the country, and her father carried her to an island off the coast of Italy, where she was free to practice her enchantments to her heart's content.

This same Ulysses of whom you read in connection with the Lotus-Eaters and the Lotus flowers, on his return from the Trojan War, visited the island of the wonderful

NIGHTSHADE.

Circe. The companions of Ulysses had gone upon the island first, and finding everything there so beautiful and comfortable, had abandoned themselves to idleness and pleasure and were changed by Circe's enchantments into swine. Ulysses, who was fortified against all charms by a little herb given him by Mercury, went to the sorceress, sword in hand, and demanded the restoration of his companions in arms. She not only complied with his demands, but welcomed him so very cordially, that for a whole year, the hero forgot his glory and himself dwelt on the island of the enchantress. This is only a fable, children, but one of those fables that wise men find much truth in, and which you will comprehend when you are older.

# The Oak and the Mistletoe Seed.

A SEED of the beautiful mistletoe was separated from its parent. It went forth in search of a home wherein it might receive protection and care. "Perhaps," said the little seed to itself, "I may one day be a large and beautiful plant like that from which I have sprung."

It knew by instinct that the earth, in whose bosom the mighty forest trees buried their spreading roots, would have no welcome for a seed of mistletoe; that it must seek elsewhere the rest and nourishment it so desired. "Surely there must be room for me in the world!" the wandering seed exclaimed.

Seeing a stately elm, it thought, "Here is a tree that must be as generous as he is stately, here shall be my home." But the elm was not generous. He scorned the humble petition of the seed, and said there was not a corner in his branches for a beggar. In vain did the seed plead its great need of help; the elm was as hard as a stone, and cared not at all for the tiny creature's sorrow.

A beech nearby was even more narrow-minded than the elm, and fairly drove the seed away with the angry question: "Why should I afford a resting place to vagrant shrubs of your kind?" And the poor, weary wanderer began to think that it would be as well to die at once as to die at the end of a long and fruitless pursuit.

An oak in the forest, to whom the seed next appealed, listened to the sorrowing voice of the wanderer, and was more merciful than the elm or the beech had been. Satisfied at last, the little seed found rest in the arms of the mighty oak. Before long, a delicate green leaf appeared, and then another and another; and in time, a beautiful shrub grew upon the great forest tree.

When the summer had passed, the winds of autumn came moaning through the woods, and the leaves fell in showers. The stately elm lost its beautiful foliage, the beech stood bare and shivering in the blast, and even the hospitable oak saw his splendid drapery of green change and fall. And soon the winter's ice and snow made the forest desolate. Yet was the oak grand and attractive still.

The mistletoe covered the broad bosom of the tree, and was indeed life in the midst of death. Strong and evergreen, the winter could not rob it of its beauty or its strength. Its waxen berries, rivaling the snow in whiteness, seemed to the beech and elm like so many mocking eyes turned upon them. But to the venerable oak, they were like rare and precious jewels.

One fine day in winter, the oak made this speech to a merry little group who stood admiring the mistletoe: "When I received a tiny, stray seed and gave it my protection, do you suppose that I knew what would follow? If I had stood in the forest destitute of leaves as my fellow trees are, would you have gathered around to admire me?

"I know that the mistletoe, with its white berries, attracted your eyes, yet am I not proud to bear that shrub in my arms and call it my foster child? Kindness enriches both the giver and the receiver. In my long, long life, I have learned many lessons, but this is the best of all: be kind for the very sake of kindness, and you will have your reward."

---

## A SUMMER LONGING.

I MUST away to wooded hills and vales,
    Where broad, slow streams flow cool and
silently,
And idle barges flap their listless sails.
    For me, the summer sunset glows and pales,
And green fields wait for me.

I long for shadowy forests, where the birds
    Twitter and chirp at noon from every tree;
I long for blossomed leaves and lowing herds;
And Nature's voices say in mystic woods,
    "The green fields wait for thee."

I dream of uplands, where the primrose shines
    And waves her yellow lamps above the lea;
Of tangled copses, swung with trailing vines;
Of open vistas, skirted with tall pines,
    Where green fields wait for me.

I think of long, sweet afternoons, when I
    May lie and listen to the distant sea,
Or hear the breezes in the reeds that sigh,
Or insect voices chirping shrill and dry,
    In fields that wait for me.

These dreams of summer come to bid me find
    The forest's shade, the wild bird's melody,
While summer's rosy wreaths for me are twined,
While summer's fragrance lingers on the wind,
    And green fields wait for me.

- GEORGE ARNOLD.

# The Poppy and the Corn Flower.

THERE was once a king's daughter whose name was Papava. This is an odd-sounding name, you will think; but it means *Poppy*, and the little princess was so-called because she wore always such a bright red silk dress - as red and as bright as the beautiful garden poppy.

But though Papava was so richly clad, she had not a kind heart. She was vain and selfish, not tender towards her little maids or towards the other little children in her kingdom.

"We are the richest and the greatest people in the land," she would say, tossing her proud little head.

Such beautiful things as this child had. Every morning her glossy hair was combed with a comb of gold, at mid-day she ate from a golden plate and drank from a golden cup; her toys were of gold - even her little nightrobe was of rich purple velvet trimmed with a golden cord and with golden buttons.

One day, seeing the reapers at work in the fields outside her palace grounds, she said to her sweet, gentle little waiting-maid, "Let us go out into the fields!"

The little waiting-maid bowed her head obediently as a little waiting-maid should do, and forth they went through the palace gates.

The reapers, when they saw the little Papava, all bowed

respectfully to her as is the custom in these countries where the people reverence their king and all that belong to him.

The little Papava tossed her proud head and sneered at the honest workmen who bowed so respectfully before her.

The little maid, so pretty in her simple little blue gown, smiled kindly upon the workmen, and here and there dropped a kind word to those who spoke to her.

Now a big, black cloud appeared in the far-off horizon. "A storm is coming! A storm is coming!" cried the little princess. "Here, you people," called she rudely to the workmen, "build me a shelter quick. I am the princess! Build me a house from your sheaves!"

The workmen hastened to obey. One old peasant, bowing low before the princess, said, "Pardon me, gracious princess, but there will be no shower. See, the clouds have broken, and already between the parting shines the beautiful sun."

"How dare you," screamed the princess, "refuse to do my bidding."

Then the workmen, sad that they must waste their precious sheaves just for a childish whim. Gladly would they have laid down their lives for the princess had it been necessary - but to lose their sheaves, every grain of which was of such value to them in the long winter to come - that was hard indeed!

Sadly enough, the peasants worked to build the little

house. Sheaves for the floor, sheaves for the roof, sheaves for the walls.

The little maid's eyes shone with tears - for she knew all too well of the little children, so many of them in the village, who by-and-by, when the cold winter came, would need the food that these wasted, ruined sheaves might bring them.

But Papava's proud head was high, she stamped her little velvet-covered feet in rage, a rage all unbecoming, had she but known it, to a little royal princess.

At last the house was done. "Come in," said she sharply to her little maid.

Outside the sun was shining warmly, brightly. But, suddenly, without one second's warning, a great flash of lightning, an awful roar and crash of thunder, and the little house of sheaves fell in flames about the heads of the proud little princess and her little maid. Nothing could save them. O, it was a sad, sad sight.

Awe-struck, paralyzed with fear, the peasants gazed upon the burning grain. How it crackled and snapped! No one could approach it so intense and terrible was the heat.

By-and-by the flames died away; nothing was left but a heap of burning ashes, covering over the charred, burned bodies of the little children.

Sad, speechless, the reapers went back to their work. Only the old reaper - the one who had begged the little princess to spare the sheaves to them - went to the palace to tell to the king and queen the sad, sad story.

The parents, broken-hearted, realized all too late that

their own unwise love, their own mistaken teaching, had helped to make their child the selfish, willful child that she was, that it was their pride, their indulgence that had brought the little princess to her death.

The following summer, when the corn stood golden in the field, from out the heap of ashes, sprang the beautiful little blue cornflower, and close beside it the proud red poppy.

"Truly these sprang from the ashes of the children," said the reapers, "the little cornflower is the little maid; the proud poppy is the little princess."

By-and-by, the winds caught up the seeds of the poppy and of the cornflower and scattered them over the fields; and so every year the seeds were blown farther and farther, until the little flowers are seen now over all the countries in the world where the poppy and the cornflower can grow - standing as they do, typical of sin and innocence - gentle, loving kindness and haughty, cruel pride.

---

## OUR WILLOWS.

IT is when the east wind blows,
    And his cohorts gather and ride,
That the willows before my window
    Show me their silver side.

When the air is sweet and still,
    And all heaven beams light and mirth,
Though their green boughs quiver and sparkle,
    They look and lean to earth.
But the moment the storm-wind blows,
    And the storm-clouds gather and ride,

They lift up their branches to heaven,
    And show me the *silver* side.

'Tis not to fear and sadness,
    They owe that silver sheen;
Unseen, in calm and gladness,
    *It underlies the green.*
And when the Northwest triumphs,
    And baffled storm-clouds flee,
They fling out their silvery streamers,
    *And hail the* victory.

- HOURS AT HOME

------

# The Transplanted Flower.

EVERY time that a good child dies, one of God's angels comes down to earth and takes the dead child in his arms, then spreads his large white wings and flies over all the spots which the child best loved and plucks a whole handful of flowers, which he carries up to the Almighty, that they may bloom in still greater loveliness in heaven than they did upon earth; and the Almighty presses all such flowers upon His heart, but He gives a kiss to the one He prefers, and then the flower becomes endowed with a voice, and can join the choir of the blessed. These words were spoken by one of God's angels, as he carried up a dead child to heaven, and the child heard him as in a dream and they passed over the spots in his home where the little one had played, and they passed through gardens filled with beautiful flowers.

"Which shall we take with us and transplant into the kingdom of heaven?" asked the angel.

There stood a slender, lovely rose-bush, only some wicked hand had broken the stem, so that all its sprigs, loaded with half-open buds, were withering around.

"Poor rose-bush!" said the child; "let's take it, in order that it may be able to bloom above, in God's kingdom."

And the angel took it and kissed the child for its kind intention, and the little one half-opened its eyes. They plucked some of the gay, ornamental flowers, but took likewise the despised buttercup and wild pansy.

"Now we have plenty of flowers," said the child, and the angel nodded assent; but he did not yet fly upward to God. It was night, and all was quiet; they remained in the large town, and hovered over one of the narrow streets, where lay heaps of straw, ashes, and sweepings - for, being quarter-day, there had been several removals. There lay fragments of plates, pieces of plaster-of-Paris, rags, and old hats, and all sorts of things that become shabby.

And amidst this confused heap, the angel pointed to the broken fragments of a flower-pot, and to a lump of mold that had fallen out of it, and was kept together by the roots of a large, withered field-flower, which, being worthless, had been flung into the street.

"We will take it with us," said the angel, "and I will tell you why as we fly along."

And as they flew, the angel related as follows:

"In your narrow street, a poor, sickly boy lived in a lonely cellar. He had been bedridden from his childhood. In his best days, he could just walk on crutches up and down the room a couple of times, but that was all. During some days in summer, the sun just shone for about half an hour on the floor of the cellar, and when the poor boy sat and warmed himself in its beams, and he saw the red blood through his delicate fingers that he held before his face, then he considered that he had been abroad that day. All he knew of the forest and its beautiful spring verdure was from the first green sprig of beech that his neighbor's son used to bring him, and he would hold it over his head and dream that he was under the beech trees, amid the sunshine and the carol of birds.

"One spring day, the neighbor's boy brought him some field flowers besides, and among them, there happened to be one that still retained its root, which he therefore carefully planted in a flowerpot and placed in the window near his bed. The flower was planted by a lucky hand; it thrived and put forth new shoots and blossomed every year. It became the rarest flower garden for the sick boy, and his only little treasure here on earth; he watered it, cherished it, and took care that it should profit by every sunbeam, from the first to the last, that filtered through that lonely window, and the flower became interwoven in his very dreams: for it was for him it bloomed; for him it spread its fragrance and delighted the eye, and it was to the flower he turned in the last gasp of death when the Lord called him.

"He has now been a year with his heavenly Father, and for a year did the flower stand forgotten in the window until it withered. It was therefore cast out among the sweepings in the street on the day of moving; and this is the flower, the poor faded flower, which we have added to our nosegay because this flower gave more joy than the rarest flower in the garden of a queen."

"And how do you know all this?" asked the child as the angel carried him up to heaven.

"I know it," said the angel, "because I myself was the little sick boy who walked upon crutches; and I know my own flower."

And the child opened his eyes completely and looked full at the angel's serenely beautiful countenance; and at the same moment, they had reached the kingdom of heaven, where all was joy and blessedness.

And God pressed the dead child to His heart, where he obtained wings like the other angel, and flew hand in hand with him; and God pressed all the flowers to His heart, but kissed the poor withered field flower, which then became endowed with a voice and joined in the chorus of angels that surrounded the Almighty, some of whom are quite near their heavenly Father, while others are standing outside them in a large circle, and others again beyond these, and so on, further and still further, in endless succession, but all equally happy. And they all sang, great and little, the good, blessed child, and the poor field flower that lay withered and cast away amongst the sweepings, under the rubbish of a moving day, in the narrow dingy street.

- HANS ANDERSON.

## THE BLUE-BELL.

THERE is a story I have heard —
A poet learned it from a bird,
And kept its music, every word —

A story of a dim ravine,
O'er which the towering treetops lean,
With one blue rift of sky between.

And there, two thousand years ago,
A little flower, as white as snow,
Swayed in the silence to and fro.

Day after day, with longing eye,
The floweret watched the narrow sky
And fleecy clouds that floated by.

And through the darkness, night by night,
One gleaming star would climb the height,
And cheer the lonely floweret's sight.

Thus, watching the blue heavens afar,
And the rising of its favorite star,
A slow change came, but not to mar;

For softly o'er its petals white
There crept a blueness like the light
Of skies upon a summer's night.

And in its chalice, I am told,
The bonny bell was found to hold
A tiny star that gleamed like gold.

And blue-bells of the Scottish land
Are loved on every foreign strand
Where stirs a Scottish heart or hand.

Now, little people, sweet and true,
I find a lesson here for you,
Writ in the floweret's bell of blue:

The patient child whose watchful eye
Strives after all things pure and high
Shall take their image by and by.

------

Small service is true service while it lasts;
    Of humblest friends, bright creature! scorn not one,
The daisy, by the shadow that it casts,
    Protects the lingering dew-drop from the sun.

## Golden Rod and Aster.

THE golden days of Indian Summer were upon us! Such dreamy, hazy days!

Our teacher has sent us in search of the Sabbatia or American Centaury.

"You will find one kind, the stellaris, in the marshy meadows, I am sure," she had said, "in just such places as you found the Arethusias in the spring."

We had a long search for it, and were about to give it up and report, "Not indigenous to the Rosedale soil," when a shout from Ned, in among the cat-tails and the Bur-weeds, told us the flower was found.

And it was well worth the search! Their smooth stems, their bitter juice, their entire leaves without stipules; their regular flowers, their one-celled and many-seeded capsule told us they might plainly be placed with the Gentian work.

Our specimen, the Sabbatia stellaris, had a slightly angular stem with long, one-flowered branches. The leaves were sharp and lance-shaped, the calyx and corolla each five-parted. The large, pink flowers with the yellow star in the center, bordered with red, were indeed beautiful. Such odd grass-like leaves as the upper leaves were. Nothing like them had been seen in any other plants!

This was almost our last flower lesson, and we had much the feeling that there never would be another sunshine in all our lives.

"November, December, January, February, March — five whole months before the spring flowers come again," said Allie. "O dear, I wonder why we have flowers only half the year. I know I shall just hate this winter."

"There is just the loveliest story about that very thing — the flowers only half the year," said Fannie. "I read it from Hawthorne's 'Twice Told Tales', only yesterday. I'll bring the book to school, and perhaps our teacher will read it to us after we have analyzed our flowers."

"Indeed she will," said our teacher herself, suddenly appearing beneath a great tree by the roadside, where, with her arms full of Golden Rod and Aster, she had stopped to rest.

"We found the American Centaury! We found it!" cried Ned. "Pink flowers, yellow eye, with the red edges — just as you said!"

"Yes, indeed, this is it! Let's sit down here in the shade and look at it; and I want you to notice these Golden Rods.

I have three or four kinds here, and there are more than fifty in America.

"We cannot do much with the Golden Rod or the Aster either; for they are Composite. Who remembers some of the distinguishing points of the Compositae?"

"Five united anthers!" said Ned.

GOLDEN ROD.

"Dense heads of flowers!" said Harry.

"Fruit always an achene!" said Allie.

"And what is an achene, Allie?"

"A dry cell with one seed in it!" answered Allie promptly.

"Can't catch Allie on flower lore," said Harry proudly, looking at his dainty little sister.

"Now in the Golden Rod, we see at once the little flowers or florets are tubular. And the heads have little rays. Five or six of them — never more than twelve. Look carefully at the base of the flowers, and you will find little hairs or bristles there.

"That is called the pappus, which means 'grandfather gray-beard.' Those little hairs are all the calyx the composite flowers have, and these vary greatly in their form and size.

"In the Dandelion and Thistle, you know how this increases in size while the fruit is ripening until, at last, it becomes a feathery tail which wafts away the seeds. This pappus as you see it on the dandelion, may well be called the 'ghost of the flowers.'

"Now let us see about the color of the rays."

"They are yellow!"

"And how many rows?"

"One row!"

"Now, are the scales of the little involucre of the same length?"

"The outer ones are shorter!"

"Are there few or many florets in a head, and what is the color of the pappus?"

AMERICAN CANTAURY.

"There are few florets, and the pappus is white!"

"Are the leaves alternate or opposite?"

"The leaves are alternate!"

"All this brings us at once to the Solidago, the true name of the Golden Rod.

"These beautiful Purple Asters, together with the Golden Rod, seem the most beautiful flowers of the whole year. And they are so generous, blowing everywhere and for everybody. We find them in the woods and by the wayside; in rocky pastures and in green meadows; always with their bright dresses and shining faces like the stars whose namesakes they are."

As we examine them, we find that like the Solidago, each flower is composed of numerous small ones; those of the disk tubular and perfect; those of the ray with only pistils. There are many kinds of Asters — that you all know. And they are so beautiful! It seems cruel for Old Jack Frost to put an end to all this autumn glory. Still, we can comfort ourselves that he cannot kill either the asters or the Golden Rod. They will only go to sleep for a while and be all the brighter after their nap.

---

"O Columbine! open your folded wrapper,
Where two twin turtle-doves dwell;
O cuckoo-pint! toll me the purple clapper
That hangs in your clear, green bell."

# Why the Flowers Bloom

only Half the Year.

MOTHER Ceres was exceedingly fond of her daughter Proserpina and seldom let her go alone into the fields. But just at the time when my story begins, the good lady was very busy because she had the care of the wheat, and the Indian corn, and the rye and barley, and, in short, of the crops of every kind all over the world; and as the season thus far had been unusually backward, it was necessary to make the harvest ripen more speedily than usual.

"Dear mother," said Proserpina, "I shall be very lonely while you are away. May I not run down to the seashore and ask some of the nymphs to come up out of the waves and play with me?"

"Yes, child," answered Mother Ceres. "The sea nymphs are good creatures and will never lead you into any harm. But you must take care not to stray away from them, and go wandering about the fields by yourself. Young girls without their mothers to take care of them are apt to get into mischief." The child promised to be as prudent as if she were a grown-up woman, and by the time the winged dragon had whirled the car out of sight, she was already on the shore, calling to the sea nymphs to come and play with her.

By way of showing her joy, the child asked them to go with her a little way into the fields, to gather an abundance of flowers, with which she would make each of her playmates a wreath. "Oh no, dear Proserpina," cried the sea nymphs, "we dare not go with you upon the dry land. We are apt to grow faint unless at every breath we can sniff up the salt breeze of the ocean."

"It is a great pity," said Proserpina. "But do you wait for me here, and I will run and gather my apron full of flowers and be back again before the surf wave has broken ten times over you."

"We will wait, then," answered the sea nymphs. "But while you are gone, we may as well lie down on a soft sponge under the water." The young Proserpina ran quickly to a spot where only the day before she had seen many flowers. Soon her apron was filled and brimming over with blossoms; when suddenly seeing a large shrub covered with magnificent flowers, she seized it and pulled and pulled; but was hardly able to loosen the soil about its roots. Again she pulled with all her might, and noticed that the earth began to crack and stir to some distance around the stem. She pulled a third time but relaxed her hold, thinking she heard a rumbling sound beneath her feet. Laughing at herself for so childish a notion, she made another effort; up came the shrub, and Proserpina staggered back, surprised at the deep hole which its roots had left in the soil.

Much to her astonishment, the hole kept growing larger, and deeper and deeper, until it really seemed to have no bottom; and all the while, there came a rumbling noise out of its depths, louder and louder, nearer and nearer, and sounding like the tramp of horses' hoofs and the rattling of wheels. Too frightened to run away, she waited and soon saw a team of four sable horses, snorting smoke out of their nostrils, and tearing away out of the earth with a splendid golden chariot whirling at their heels.

In the chariot sat the figure of a man richly dressed, with a crown on his head, all flaming with diamonds. He was rather handsome, but looked sullen and discontented; and he kept rubbing his eyes and shading them with his hand, as if the light of the sun pained them.

"Do not be afraid," said he, with as cheerful a smile as he knew how to put on. "Come! Will you not like to ride a little way with me, in my beautiful chariot?"

But Proserpina was so alarmed, that she cried, "Mother, Mother Ceres! Come quickly and save me."

"Why should you be so frightened, my pretty child?" said he, trying to soften his rough voice. "I promise you not to do you any harm. What! You have been gathering flowers? Wait till we come to my palace and I will give you a garden full of prettier flowers than those, all made of pearls, diamonds, and rubies. Can you guess who I am? They call me Pluto, and I am king of diamonds and all other precious stones."

"Let me go home!" screamed Proserpina, "let me go home."

"My home is better than your mother's," answered King Pluto. "It is a palace all made of gold, with crystal windows; and because there is little or no sunshine, the palace is illuminated with diamond lamps."

"I don't care for golden palaces and thrones," sobbed Proserpina, "Oh, my mother, my mother! Carry me back to my mother!"

But King Pluto, as he called himself, only shouted to his steeds to go faster. "Pray do not be foolish, Proserpina," said he, in rather a sullen tone. "I offer you my palace and my crown, and all the riches that are under the earth; and you treat me as if I was doing you an injury. Pray let me see you smile."

"Never!" answered Proserpina, "I shall never smile again till you set me down at my mother's door."

But she might just as well have talked to the wind that whistled past them; for Pluto urged on his horses and went faster and faster than ever.

At last, they came to the palace of King Pluto which was illuminated by means of large precious stones that seemed to burn like so many lamps.

Pluto summoned his servants and bade them spread a feast; and above all things, not to fail to bring a golden beaker of the water of Lethe for Proserpina.

"Only drink a little of it, and you will cease to grieve for your mother and be perfectly happy in my palace," said King Pluto.

"I will neither drink that nor anything else," said Proserpina. "Nor will I taste a morsel of food, even if you keep me forever here."

"I should be sorry for that," replied Pluto, patting her cheek; for he really wished to be kind if he had only known how. "You are a spoiled child, I perceive, my little Proserpina; but when you see the nice things which my cook will make for you, your appetite will quickly come back again."

Then, sending for the head cook, he gave orders that

all sorts of nice things should be set before Proserpina. He had a secret motive in this for, you are to understand, it is a fixed law, that when persons are carried off to the land of magic, if they only taste any food there, they can never get back to their friends.

But my story must now clamber out of King Pluto's dominions and see what Mother Ceres has been about since she was bereft of her daughter.

You remember Proserpina gave a loud scream just as she was being borne away in the chariot, out of sight and hearing.

This shriek was heard by Mother Ceres, but she had mistaken the rumbling of the chariot wheels for a peal of thunder and imagined that a shower was coming up, that would assist in making the corn grow. But at the sound of Proserpina's shriek, she started and looked about in every direction, not knowing whence it came, but feeling almost certain that it was her daughter's voice.

So she quickly left the field in which she had been so busy; and, as her work was not half done, the grain looked, the next day, as if it needed both sun and rain, and as if it were blighted in the ear, and had something the matter with its roots.

"Where is Proserpina?" cried Ceres. "Where is my child? Tell me, you naughty sea-nymphs, have you enticed her under the sea?"

"Oh no, good Mother Ceres," said the innocent nymphs, "We never should dream of such a thing. Proserpina has been at play with us, but it was a long time ago. She went up on to the dry land to gather some flowers for a wreath."

Ceres waited to hear no more but hurried off to make inquiries all through the neighborhood. But nobody told her anything that could enable the poor woman to guess what had become of Proserpina.

Poor Mother Ceres! So much did she suffer that her face once so young-looking, grew to look like an elderly person in a very short time.

She cared not how she dressed, nor had she thought of flinging away the wreath of withered poppies, which she put on the very morning of her daughter's disappearance.

She roamed about in such a wild manner that people took her for some distracted person, never dreaming that she could be Mother Ceres, who had the oversight of every seed which the husbandman planted.

Nowadays, however, she gave herself no trouble about seed-time nor harvest but left the farmers to take care of their own affairs, and the crops to fade or flourish, as the case might be.

But what has been happening all this time in Pluto's kingdom?

"My own little Proserpina," he used to say, "I wish you could like me a little better. We gloomy and cloudy-natured persons have often as warm hearts at bottom as those of a more cheerful character."

"Ah!" said Proserpina, "you should have tried to make me like you before carrying me off. Now you had better let me go again. Then I might remember you sometimes, and think that you were as kind as you knew how to be. Perhaps someday I might come back, and pay you a visit."

"No, no," answered Pluto with his gloomy smile, "I will not trust you for that. You are too fond of living in the broad daylight, and gathering flowers. Are not these gems that I have ordered for you prettier than a violet?"

"Not half so pretty," said Proserpina, snatching the gems from Pluto's hand and flinging them to the other end of the hall. "Oh, my sweet violets, shall I never see you again?"

Now it happened that just here one of Pluto's servants came in bringing to Proserpina a little pomegranate from her own world above.

As soon as Proserpina saw the pomegranate, she told the servant he had better take it away. "I shall not touch it, I assure you," said she. "If I were ever so hungry, I should never think of eating such a dry, miserable pomegranate as that."

"It is the only one in the world," said the servant.

He set down the golden salver with the dry pomegranate upon it and left the room.

"At least, I may smell it," thought Proserpina.

So she took up the pomegranate and applied it to her nose; and so great was the temptation that before she knew what she was about the fruit found its way into her mouth. Just as she had bitten into it the door of the room opened and in came King Pluto followed by Quicksilver, who had been urging him to let his prisoner go.

"My little Proserpina," said the King, sitting down and

drawing her to him, "here is Quicksilver who tells me a great many misfortunes have happened to innocent people on account of my keeping you in my kingdom. And an iron heart I should have, indeed, if I could detain you here any longer, my poor child, when it is now six months since you have tasted food. I give you your liberty. Go with Quicksilver. Hasten home to your dear mother."

During all this time, Mother Ceres had been sitting disconsolately at home, with her torch burning in her hand. She had been idly watching the flame, when, all at once, it flickered and went out. "What does this mean?" thought she. "It was an enchanted torch, and should have kept burning till my child came back."

Lifting her eyes she was surprised to see a sudden verdure flashing over the brown and barren fields, just as you may have seen a golden hue gleaming across the landscape, from the just risen sun.

"Does the earth disobey me?" exclaimed Mother Ceres, indignantly. "Does it presume to be green when I have bidden it be barren until my daughter shall be returned to my arms?"

"Then open your arms, dear mother," cried a well-known voice, "and take your little daughter into them."

Their mutual joy and happiness is not to be described. When their hearts had grown a little more quiet, Mother Ceres looked anxiously at Proserpina.

"My child," said she, "did you taste any food while you were in King Pluto's palace?"

"Dearest mother," answered the child, "I will tell you

the whole truth. Until this very morning, not a morsel of food had passed my lips. But today, they brought me a pomegranate (a dry, miserable one) and having seen no fruit for so long, and I was so faint with hunger, I was tempted just to bite it. The instant I tasted it Quicksilver and King Pluto came into the room. I had not swallowed a morsel; but - dear mother, I hope it was no harm - but six of the pomegranate seeds, I am afraid, remained in my mouth."

"Ah, unfortunate child and miserable me!" exclaimed Ceres. "For each of those six seeds you must spend one month of every year in King Pluto's palace. You are but half restored to your mother. Only six months with me, and six with that good-for-nothing King of Darkness."

"Do not speak so harshly of poor King Pluto," said Proserpina, kissing her mother. "He has some very good qualities. He certainly did wrong to carry me off, but then, as he says, it is but a dismal sort of life for him to live all alone in that great gloomy place; and it has made a wonderful change in his actions to have a little girl running up and down stairs in his home. There is some comfort in making him happy, and so let us be thankful that he did not keep me the whole year round."

- NATHANIEL HAWTHORNE, *from "Pomegranate Seed."*

## DAISY NURSES

The daisies white are nursery maids,
    With frills upon their caps;
And daisy buds are little babies
    They tend upon their laps.
Sing Heigh ho! while the wind sweeps low,
Both nurses and babies are nodding — just so.

The daisy babies never cry,
    The nurses never scold;
They never crush the dainty frills
    About their cheeks of gold.
But prim and white in gay sunlight
They're nid-nid-nodding — a pretty sight!

The daisies love the golden sun,
    Up in the clear blue sky;
He gazes kindly down at them,
    And winks his joyful eye,
While soft and slow, all in a row,
Both nurses and babies are nodding — just so.

------

# Golden Rod and Aster

## A FAIRY TALE

A LONG, long while ago, there lived upon the top of
a great hill a very old woman, bent and crooked and
crabbed by the weight of many years that lay upon her.
Up there, one would have thought that she would have
kept herself gladsome and happy in spite of the years
or the old age creeping on; for the birds were so merry,
and the sun shone so brightly, and everything rejoiced

in the brightness and beauty about them; all except the old woman, who borrowed her looks from nothing there, unless it was the gray sky when the rain fell. Perhaps it was living alone so much that brought it about, for she had only herself to think of, and thinking of one's self will bring neither smiles to the face nor gladness to the heart. At any rate, she grew more and more morose each year, and the sky was not blue for her; and the sun shone only to scorch her garden's good, while the birds' merry songs were lost upon her.

The house grew older, like its mistress, as the years went on, and promised to fall down before many more seasons should come and go. But in a certain spot where the moss was green and the shade cool and sweet, a delightful spring burst forth, and went gurgling and dripping and tumbling down the stony side of the hill, until, meeting another farther down, the two made a pretty brook, noisy in its glee, where the birds came to dip, and coo, and comb their feathers. The brook danced far down into the valley, and children played about its brink. But they rarely ventured up the hillside whence it started, for a certain fame of the old woman had gone abroad through the valley.

It was a question whether it was a good thing to grow famous in such a way as this, for the old woman's power, it was said, lay in being able to change beasts into creeping things, and birds into beasts, and children into whatsoever she willed. No wonder, then, that children avoided her and her home, and even the red-cheeked apples upon her ancient trees.

One day there were seen, following the course of the brook, two bright-faced little children, hand-in-hand, stepping from stone to stone, or stopping gleefully to set their green treasures afloat upon its waters; their tongues joyously busy, or their voices gay with song and laughter. Every now and then they stopped to rest in the shade, and gather a new store of moss and leaves, and dropping nuts, whose cups made little vessels from which to drink.

How they laughed as a gray squirrel peeped at them from a hole in the hollow trunk of the oak tree bending above the stream!

Sitting down within the shadow of the hill they rested, and began to eat the cakes the elder set upon her knee. Her golden hair fell soft and thick about her neck, and the sunshine and shadow playing upon it made beautiful shades of shifting color come and go, while her bright little face fairly shone with good humor. Her companion was smaller, with a more delicate outline of feature, and large, soft eyes, that were beautiful in their very depth.

They spread the few bright leaves they had gathered upon the sod, and as the younger, weaving them skillfully into a tiny wreath, crowned the golden head of the elder, their merry laughter awoke the echoes among the hills.

There was a curious haze upon the air, and when the wind stirred the boughs overhead, the acorns dropped about their feet. In the fields beyond, the yellow corn hung where the leaves rustled with every breath, and the crows flew, cawing overhead. Away up above the hill the apples hung, russet and yellow and red, or fell in mellow heaps upon the sod.

"We are almost there," the elder said, hopefully, "only the hill to climb now."

"But you are not afraid?" half doubtfully, questioned the younger, fearing that the old woman was hidden somewhere close at hand, and might pounce upon them at any moment.

"Afraid? oh, no; I will be so glad to ask her how we may do the good we wish, or become a joy to someone or everyone. They tell me she is very powerful: and can make people as they wish to be, that is, if it so pleases her."

"But suppose she is cross and old, and, may be, wicked, too, let us go back, Golden Hair; do let us go back."

"Oh, no," again answered the cheery voice of the elder, "not now, when we are so near. See, we have only to climb a little farther."

At this they went on their way, singing a song that was of the good they would do if they could. The meaning was so wrought into their singing that a new courage came to them.

Now, the old woman was spinning that afternoon, in front of her door. She wasn't in a very good humor, for her last bit of flax was about all gone, and she did not exactly know where to get any more. So what does she see but the two children coming up the slope in front of her, hand-in-hand, singing gaily as they came, and only stopping for a moment at the spring to drink, and gather each a russet apple from the heaps upon the ground.

She pounced upon them in a moment; and with the wrinkles gathered in a mass between her eyes, making her look very fierce indeed, and her cap somewhat awry, brought their song suddenly to an end.

"Goodness, gracious me! Whom have we here, drinking at my spring and taking apples that are not their own?"

Golden Hair spoke first.

"Pray forgive us for the wrong, if we did any; we are looking for the woman upon the hill who can give us what we wish, or change us into what we wish, or change us into what we would like to be."

"Indeed," said the old woman.

"We wish for the good that will make all others happy," said sweet Soft Eyes.

"Indeed," said the old woman again.

"Can you give it to us?" from Golden Hair.

"Bless my soul," said the old woman, "but here are two simpletons; to make others happy, indeed; ha! ha!"

"Don't you like to do it, yourself, then?" from Soft Eyes. "Oh, Golden Hair, she isn't the one we want to see?"

"Ah, then you can tell us where she lives, please," from Golden Hair, "and here are the apples, and we are sorry to have vexed you."

"I'll show you, oh, yes; just come in and sit awhile and you can have the piece of pie that is spoiling upon the shelf."

The children, not liking to disobey her wishes, went half in fear within the door and sat down.

That was a long, long time ago, and those who saw the two pretty children go up the hill could not remember to have seen them come down again but it was remarkable that from that time on there came a new bloom everywhere; tall branches of lovely field flowers that swayed and tossed gaily in the wind or flung out golden glories of color to make every heart glad that saw them.

Some wondered, others admired, and all loved the new-comers, and every heart was made happier for their coming. They came in time to be called, by those who loved them, Golden Rod and Aster, and always where one was found the other would surely be close at hand.

Do the little folks who may read this, wonder, with me, if the two pretty children, Golden Hair and Soft Eyes, were really changed by the old woman's magic wand into the beautiful laughing Golden Rod and her twin sister, soft-eyed Aster? I, for one, almost believe it.

- HELEN KERN.

## GOLDEN ROD

HOW in the world did I happen to bloom
    All by myself alone,
By the side of a dusty, country road,
    With only a rough old stone

"For company?" And the golden-rod,
    As she drooped her yellow head,
Gave a mournful sigh. "Who cares for me,
    Or knows I'm alive?" she said.

"A snow-white daisy I'd like to be,
    Half hid in the cool green sod:
Or a pink spirea, or sweet wild rose —
    But I'm *only a golden-rod.*

"Nobody knows that I'm here, nor cares
    Whether I live or die.
Lovers of beautiful flowers, who wants
    Such a common thing as I?"

But all of a sudden she ceased her plaint,
    For a child's voice cried in glee,
"Here's a dear little lovely golden-rod!
    Did you bloom on purpose for me?

"Down by the brook the tall spirea
    And the purple asters nod,
And beckon to me — but more than all
    Do I love *you,* golden-rod!"

She raised the flower to her rosy lips,
    And merrily kissed its face,
"Ah! now I see," said the golden-rod,
    "How this is the very place

"That was meant for me; and I'm glad I bloomed
    Just here by the road alone,
With nobody near for company
    But a dear old mossy stone!"

# Our Last Flower Lesson.

To our last flower lesson we brought the beautiful Sabbatias; some Golden Rod and Asters, and also some beautiful blue Gentians.

Such fun as we had that morning gathering the Gentians. Ned had been the first to find them — Ned who was always up at daybreak in the summertime searching the woods and fields.

"A surprise for our teacher!" said he as he divided his treasures among us. "I don't believe she thought the Gentians had come yet. I've been watching them down there by Willow Creek these two weeks."

"How do you know these are all Gentians?" asked Harry—the boy who always demanded the proof of things.

"Well, I don't *know*; but I think they are. To be sure these flowers are closed, these are open—still there seem to be family resemblances," answered Ned demurely.

Our teacher was indeed surprised, and delighted, too, with Ned's 'big find' as he called it. "Closed Gentians, Five-flowered Gentians, Fringed Gentians all together!" exclaimed she. "Why, Ned, this is a rare treat indeed."

"Those closed Gentians I've had at home in water two days thinking they were buds," said Ned. "I thought they would open out like the others."

"No, they never would have opened. You see, the reason

is just this," said the teacher putting on a comical expression of make-believe seriousness.

Once the Queen of the Fairies was out late at night. The midnight hour had passed and the Silver Moon, the Fairy Lamp, had swung down and out of sight. Hurrying to a Gentian, the Fairy asked for shelter.

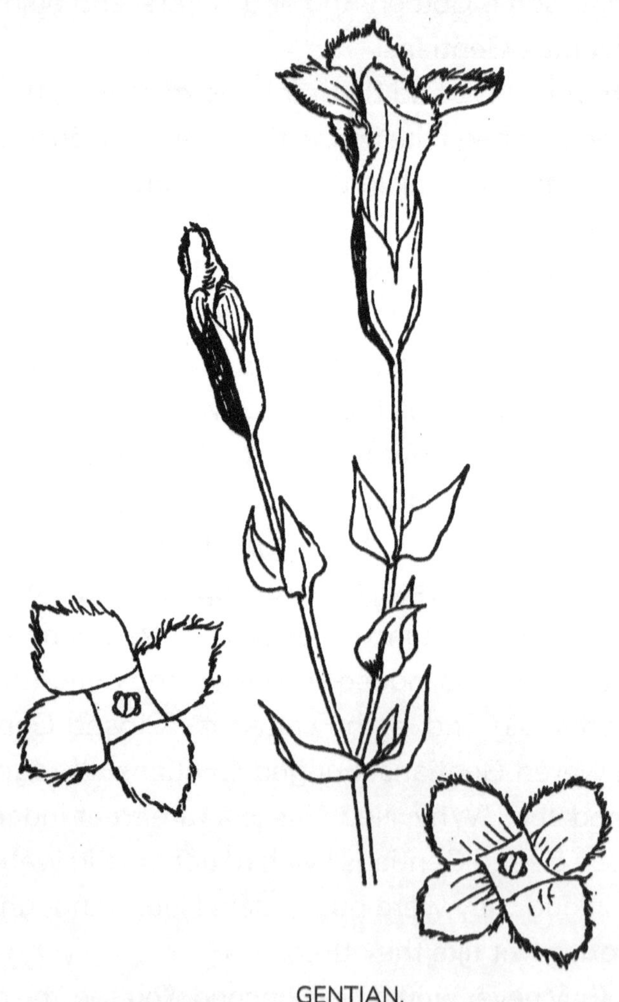

GENTIAN.

"Who are you that you disturb me at this time o' night?" called the sleepy Gentian.

"I am Queen of the Fairies," cried the belated little lady.

"Very well, then, if you are the Queen of the Fairies you can find places enough to sleep. Go away and let me sleep."

Poor little Fairy Queen! She was afraid out in the big, dark world.

"I will try again," said she. And so going up to another Gentian not far away, she timidly said, "Can you give shelter to a tired wayfarer, good flower?"

Out peeped the Gentian. "Poor little lady," said the flower. "Whoever you are, you are too little to be out in the dark. Come in and let me cover you over till the Sun comes."

Then the little tired Fairy slept soundly until morning began to dawn. Then, as she hastened away in the dim light, she said, turning to the flower that had protected her, "You, kind friend, you and all your children shall hereafter be distinguished from all other Gentians by the power which I now give you to open and receive the warm sunlight when first he peeps upon the world."

"Oh, I like that story," exclaimed Allie.

"Allie is always alive to the beautiful in the world," answered the teacher, with a fond look at the little yellow-haired, violet-eyed child.

"Let us note the closed Gentian first. It has a simple, erect stem; smooth, opposite, sharp-pointed, rather oval leaves. The flowers are in a whorl (as we have so often seen the leaves of other plants) the corolla is *ten-parted*, the inner parts folded together like a fan. I wonder if the pistil in them, shut in so close, doesn't wish he had been more generous with the little Fairy Queen!

"The five-flowered Gentian, which you found in the woods, did you not, Ned? — is smaller, you will notice at once. The corolla is bell-form, *five*-parted, and those, too, very pointed and sharp. It has a square stem branched, and the leaves clasp about it. The corolla never folds but is always open like a bell.

"And now these beautiful fringed Gentians! Was there ever anything so lovely! But dear me, we have said that of every flower since April, I think! They are all so beautiful when we come to look at them carefully that each one in its turn *does* seem the most beautiful of all!

"But this Fringed Gentian does seem almost Nature's masterpiece! So rich in color, so exquisite in form. See this delicately cut fringe; the square calyx; its parts tapering so beautifully! The stem is round and smooth, the branches curving gracefully at the base, and bearing a single, large erect flower at its summit. Bryant loved this little flower; and has written a tender little poem about it. Let us close our flower lesson with learning the verses. It will help us never to forget this little blue flower, and it will be pleasant, too, to associate it with this writer:

## THE FRINGED GENTIAN.

"Thou blossom, bright with autumn dew,
And covered with the heaven's own blue,
Thou openest when the quiet light
Succeeds the keen and frosty night.

"Thou comest not when violets lean
O'er wandering brooks and springs unseen,
Or columbines, in purple drest,
Nod o'er the ground-bird's hidden nest.

"Thou waitest late and comest alone,
When woods are bare and birds are flown,
And frosts and shortening days portend
The aged year is near its end.

"Then doth thy sweet and quiet eye
Look through its fringes to the sky,
Blue — blue — as if that sky let fall
A flower from its cerulean wall.

"I would that thus, when I shall see
The hour of death draw near to me,
Hope, blossoming within my heart,
May look to heaven as I depart."

— WILLIAM CULLEN BRYANT.

---

"O dear!" groaned Harry. "And have we nothing to do but to study these old school-books from now till next April when the flowers come again?"

"Are the school-books so very dull, Harry?" asked the teacher.

"Well — no — not so very dull — but — some way there seems to be something different in this kind of studying. It opens one's eyes! Why I've lived all my life here in this village and I had no idea there were so many kinds of flowers; and I'm sure I never thought of noticing their differences."

"Well, Harry, how would you like, since the flowers of the earth are going away from us, to spend the time while they are asleep, in studying their little sisters, the flowers of the sky?"

"The Stars! the Stars!"

"Will there be any stories about the stars?" asked Allie.

"Hundreds of them, Allie — more I think than there are about the flowers, even — real fairy stories about giants and enchanted animals — fiery dragons — golden chariots!"

"Eureka!" exclaimed Harry.

And so it was that we laid aside the study of our beautiful flowers, put back upon the book shelves our Botanies, began to borrow star books and talk largely of *Astronomy*.

# GREAT CLASSES.

**I.— ENDOGEN.** {
*Stem has its fibres in threads.*
*Leaves parallel-veined.*
*Flowers usually in threes or sixes, never in fives.*
*One cotyledon.*

**2.— EXOGEN.** {
*Stem with pith in the centre.*
*Leaves netted-veined.*
*Flowers usually in fives or fours, rarely in threes.*
*Two cotyledons.*

# ENDOGENS.

**1.— SPADIX-LIKE.** {
*Palm Family.*
*Arum Family.*
*Cat-tail Family.*
*Pickerel-weed Family.*

**2.— PETAL-LIKE.** {
*Water-plantain Family.*     *Greenbrier Family.*
*Trillium Family.*     *Colchicum Family.*
*Spider-wort Family*     *Lily Family.*
*Pickerel-weed Family.*     *Amaryllis Family.*
*Indian Cucumber-root Family.*     *Iris Family.*
*Orchis Family.*

**3.— HUSK-LIKE.** {
*Rush Family.*
*Sedge Family.*
*Grass Family.*

# EXOGENS.

*Apetalous*

*Monopetalous*

*Polypetalous*

**I.— APETALOUS.**

IN CATKINS. {
*Hop-in-the Hemp.*     *Willow.*
*Walnut.*     *Birch.*
*Nettle.*     *Sweetgale.*
*Plane Tree*

NOT IN CATKINS. {

MANY SEEDS IN A CELL. {
*Birthwort.*
*Stonecrop.*
*Pink.*
*Crowfoot.*

ONE OR TWO IN A CELL {
*Mirabilis.*     *Rose.*
*Laurel.*     *Pokeweed.*
*Nettle*     *Buckwheat*
*Buckthorn.*     *Hemp.*
*Elm.*     *Goosefoot.*
*Olive.*     *Amaranth.*
*Mezereum.*     *Maple.*
*Crowfoot.*

**2. MONO-PETALOUS.**

**COROLLA ON THE SEED-CRADLE.**

| | |
|---|---|
| Honeysuckle, | Lobelia, |
| Madder, | Gourd, |
| Campanula, | Teasel, |
| Huckleberry, | Valerian, |
| Composite, | |

**COROLLA BELOW THE SEED CRADLE.**

More Stamens than Petals,

| | |
|---|---|
| Pulse, | Camelia, |
| Fumitory, | Ebony, |
| Mallow, | Heath. |

Less Stamens than Petals,

| | |
|---|---|
| Sage or Mint, | Figwort, |
| Vervain, | Olive, |
| Broom-rape, | Jessamine |
| Bignonia, | |

Sta. and Petals the same.

| | |
|---|---|
| Leadwort, | Waterleaf, |
| Primrose, | Gentian, |
| Heath, | Plantain, |
| Milkweed, | Figwort, |
| Dogbane, | Nightshade, |
| Holly, | Convolvulus, |
| Sage or Mint, | Polymonium, |
| Borrage. | |

**STAMENS MORE THAN TEN.**

On the ovary free from corolla.

| | |
|---|---|
| Linden, | Custard apple, |
| Orange, | Magnolia, |
| St. Johnswort, | Nelumbo, |
| Cistus, | Mignonette, |
| Side-saddle, | Water-Lily, |
| Barberry, | Crowfoot, |
| Purslane, | Watershield, |
| Poppy, | Moonseed. |

On the ovary connected to corolla.

| | |
|---|---|
| Mallow, | Camellia. |

On the calyx

| | |
|---|---|
| Carolina Allspice, | Lythrum, |
| Ca tus, | Saxifrage, |
| Water-Lily, | Purslane. |
| Rose. | |

**3.— POLYPETALOUS.**

Corolla regular,

**STAMENS TEN, OR LESS THAN TEN.**

| | |
|---|---|
| Moon-seed, | Stone-crop, |
| Leadwort, | Pulse, |
| Barberry, | Heath, |
| Grapevine, | Lythrum, |
| Buckthorn, | Cress, |
| Purslane, | Fringe-tree, |
| Primrose, | Staff tree, |
| Gourd, | Sumach, |
| Currant | Pinweed, |
| Saxifrage, | Holly, |
| Eve.-Primrose, | Pink, |
| Cornel, | Passion Flower |
| Parsley, | Bladdernut, |
| Aralia, | Maple, |
| St. Johnswort, | Flax, |
| Rue, | Wood Sorrel, |
| Rose, | Geranium. |

Corolla irregular.

| | |
|---|---|
| Horse-chestnut, | Balsam, |
| Pulse, | Indian Cress |
| Violet, | Fumitory. |

# WHY THE LEAVES CHANGE THEIR COLOR.

The maple owned that she was tired of always wearing
green,
She knew that she had grown, of late, too shabby to be
seen!

The oak and beech and chestnut then deplored their
shabbiness,
And all, except the hemlock sad, were wild to change
their dress.

"For fashion-plates we'll take the flowers," the rustling
maple said.
"And like the tulip I'll be clothed in splendid gold and
red!"

"The cheerful sun-flower suits me best," the lightsome
beech replied.
"The marigold my choice shall be," the chestnut spoke
with pride.

The sturdy old oak took time to think, "I hate such glaring
hues;
The gillyflower, so dark and rich, I for my model choose."

So every tree in all the grove, except the hemlock sad,
According to its wish ere long in brilliant dress was clad.
And here they stand through all the soft and bright Octo-
ber days;
They wished to be like flowers — indeed they look huge
bouquets.